Revenge In Heels

A Papazian and Moretti Duology

Amanda Leigh

ISBN-979-8-9919436-5-9
Dorian Moore Books
www.dorianmoorebooks.com

Cover design by: Megan Moore @GraphiteGeek
Printed in the United States of America
No AI was used to write this book and I do not agree to my material being used to train AI

DEDICATION

How does it feel to be God's favorite?
-The Smuthood

It's been a year since the Moretti and Papazian families came together. While Mara and Zane have changed their territory for the better, there are still some who are angry with their new leaders, and they are bringing war to their doorstep. When Lia's life is put in danger after a night out, she's placed in the care of Enzo until her step-brother returns from a trip with Zane. While attraction between them grows, Enzo realizes he's not the only one Lia has her eye on. She's spent years being secretly in love with her step-brother, Aren. Enzo is more than willing to share, but will Aren feel the same?
While a war of attraction brews in Enzo's household, the danger at their doorstep doesn't slow, and it seems to be coming right for Lia. Will they be able to stop the war before it begins, or will Lia get caught in the crosshairs?

Tropes: Why choose, taboo step-sibling romance, mafia romance

Micro-Tropes: badass FMC, MMC with dominate personality, praise kink, and edging

Content/Trigger Warnings: violence, death, depictions of human trafficking, violence towards females (not between the main characters)

Table of Contents

1

LIA

Killing someone is surreal. It certainly didn't go how I imagined it. Not that I spend a lot of time imagining killing someone. I mean, we've all had the stray fantasy when someone really pisses us off, but to actually sit down and plan out taking a life? Not something I've done before. I'm still taken aback by the action. I mean, the blood is one thing. It... it *really* gets everywhere. It's soaking into the thin carpet at my feet, and I can feel it through my shoes. Oh god, this bastard ruined my new heels. I kick him in the side just for fucking with my night. *Dammit!* My nostrils fill with the smell of blood, which just adds a whole uncomfy feeling to every vampire movie I've ever watched. *Sexy vampires, my ass.*

Death and violence surrounded me for most of my life, but there was always a barrier between *it* and me. *Aren.* My step-brother is obsessive when it comes to my safety. Ever since I showed up at his house at sixteen with my mother, our families ready to join, he's been a shield against the ugliest parts of the world for me. He couldn't really protect me, not from the pain when our parents died, and not from being part of the *family.* My mother knew what she was marrying into, but I was never given the choice.

Aren couldn't stop me from entering the family, but he's included me in all of the decisions since our parents died. He took his father's place and pulled me up beside him, making it clear to *everyone* that we ruled together. Aren kept the leader, his uncle Erik Papazian, away from me. He made sure their men knew he'd slaughter anyone who thought to lay a hand on me, or let their gazes linger for too long. Aren has taken care of me all these years.

And how do I repay him? He goes out of town, and I decide to take advantage. A night of dancing at a club with my girlfriends seemed harmless enough. I was careful with my drinking. I broke some rules, but I wasn't stupid. I was vigilant about my surroundings, knowing that our family has a target on its back. Since Zane and my step-cousin Mara took over, joining the Moretti and Papazian families, some of the lesser gangs have made it a bit of a game to catch any of us unawares. They don't like some of the changes made over the last year - tough shit - and they've been trying to make a statement.

I'm sure the man at my feet thought I'd make for an easy target out on my own, but clearly he'd been wrong. God, why is there *so much* blood? I'd just gotten to my hotel room when he rushed me, shoved me in, and locked the door behind us. If he'd just tried to kill me, he might have gotten the upper hand. I hadn't heard him; I hadn't seen him. It was like he dropped from the sky right next to me. But he wanted to *talk*. He wanted to tell me all the dirty things he had planned for my body before taking me to show off like a little prize to his leaders.

The benefit of growing up in the family? I'm trained in how to defend myself. I have a class once a week to keep sharp, and Aren never lets me skip. My attacker gave me time to recover from my surprise, and then it was his turn to be surprised. The dagger I always keep strapped to my leg was easy enough to grab. Hitting him in the jugular hadn't been very hard either. But cleaning up all this *gods damned blood* is another thing. Zane and Aren are away, for fuck's sake.

Cold, double-edged panic stabs my center as I stare at *more fucking blood* seeping from the worthless corpse at my feet. I'm going to have to light a candle in here to try to dilute the smell before it makes me sick. Mara is still home, even though the guys are gone. I hate to disturb her, but she and her contacts can take this issue off my hands by morning. I call her and give an unlady-like sigh of relief when she answers against a yawn.

"Lia? You okay?"

"Mara, I'm *so sorry* to bother you."

"It's fine." I hear some shuffling and hear her calm her dog, Ani, before her voice becomes clearer. "What's wrong?"

We've always been on the cusp of being close. She and Aren grew up together, and he cares deeply for her and her well-being, but her father, being the complete jackass that he'd been, kept them from having a closer friendship. We connected instantly, and I knew my stepbrother and I were the only people she really had before her husband, Zane, came into the picture. In the last year, we spent far more time together, and we talk almost daily if we aren't seeing each other in person. She's actually happy for the first time since I met her. Truly happy and safe, even as the leader of two families that historically do not get along.

"Again, so sorry to bother you. But um, I may have run into one of those assholes trying to make a statement against us."

"Shit, are you okay?" I hear her moving now and rush to reassure her.

"Oh, *I'm* fine, but I made a bit of a mess." Silence fills the space before she lets out a little chuckle.

"Okay, are you safe? Where are you? Is there a chance there's more men around?"

"Well, I'll be honest, but you better not tell Aren. I didn't even hear the dude, but I don't think there is anyone else. I'm at the hotel we've been staying at, room 206."

"Perfect, as long as you're safe. Just stay there and make sure you're locked in. I'll send Enzo over with the cleaners, and he'll make sure everything is taken care of, okay?"

I groan a little at the idea of Enzo being sent my way. He's with Aren and I in the inner circle, but he and my brother tend to butt heads. Enzo is kind of a smart ass, which I sadly find entertaining in my boring life, and my amusement seems to just irritate Aren even more. Plus, Enzo is hot as hell. I hang up with my cousin so she can call him and send help.

I edge around the body and catch a glimpse of myself in the floor-length mirror. My hot pink dress now has gruesome crimson splatters across it. My hands are bloody and I'm sure if my hair wasn't pinned back it would be flaked with blood. *Gross*. Why didn't anyone ever tell me how *gross* death is? I wish I could shower, but I don't know how long Enzo will take, and being caught in a towel doesn't seem worth it. A piece of blood that already dried on my fingernail flakes off and my whole body shakes in revulsion.

Luckily, it doesn't take long before there is a soft knock at my door. I edge around the body and check the peephole before I unlock the door. There stands Enzo, second hand to the Moretti family, and hot-as-hell smart ass.

He steps in and chuckles softly. "Well done. Remind me not to get on your bad side."

"Too late for that, I think." When he turns back to me I flash a smile. His gaze rakes over me and I know he's taking in my body-hugging dress, heels, and makeup. I was dressed to catch myself a man tonight. I guess I *did* catch a man, just not in the way either of us planned.

"The crew is on their way. Were you injured?" He circles the body, avoiding the blood.

"Nope. He ruined my dress though, so that was upsetting." His hands become fists at his sides and I feel like I should be more clear. "He sprayed blood all over me when I killed him." I motion down to the gore.

That earns me a devastating grin. "I'll buy you a new one. A gift for a job well done." No man has any right to be as sexy as he is. I'm surrounded by hot men, yet I'm a born-again virgin.

"I'm packed up. Aren has some things here, too. Can we get out of here or do we have to wait? I need to get a shower ASAP." My bravado is fading the longer I'm trapped here with this body. Things could have gone differently. One wrong move on my part... I swallow past the fear that's climbing up my chest. I *killed* someone tonight. He deserved it. I'd do it again, but I *killed* him.

"I do need to stay until the crew arrives. Are you okay to take a shower real quick while we wait? I'll guard the bathroom door, and it should still be about ten or fifteen minutes before the crew gets here."

I eye the bathroom door with longing and nod. "As long as you promise not to peek, I'd kill to get out of this."

"I think you already took care of that. But I promise I'll guard the room. You'll be safe."

I look him in the eye and only feel reassurance. I grab clean clothes from my bag and then disappear through the door. I turn the water on the moment I step inside the bathroom and then strip while it warms up. Steam fills the room by the time I've taken the pins out of my hair and gotten out of my lingerie. Once I'm under the hot spray, I move quickly. I don't want to be in here when the *crew* shows up. I scrub my body until my skin is red and raw. I dry off quickly and change into a sports bra and some leggings and an oversized shirt that hangs off my shoulder. A very different look from how I usually present myself when anyone else is going to see me, but right now, I don't give a shit.

I step out of the bathroom and find Enzo sitting halfway between the front door and the bathroom door. A gun is in his hand, resting on his leg. Well fuck. He looks at me and seems unfazed by my change in appearance. "Just leave your ruined clothes in the bathroom. Show me where the rest of the stuff is and we'll get out of here. We can wait in the car for them to get here." He says before my eyes can wander back to the body. We work together to grab everything and then he follows me from the room. I have no idea how they go about getting rid of the bodies, of all that *blood,* and I don't really want to be here when it happens. Enzo takes my elbow to lead me towards where he parked his car. He says nothing as we load up the bags and I slide into the passenger seat. He checks his phone before closing me in the car and disappears back into the shadows. The moment he disappears from sight, panic really grabs me in her icy claws. I killed a man. I was attacked. I could have *died*. They are going to tell Aren what happened, and *he's* going to kill me. The little freedom I have is going to vanish into thin air. I'm going to end up like that princess locked in the tower-

"All set. You are staying with me tonight."

"What?" I startle and am greeted with a dull look from him.

"You. Are. Staying. With. Me. I'm not about to set you up in some other hotel. You have to be exhausted."

"I am." I don't think I've been this exhausted in all my life. I remember when my mother died and how I cried until there was nothing left in me. Maybe I'd been this exhausted then. I slept almost a whole day after hearing the news. "Can't you just take me to Mara?"

"No."

"Are you going to expand on that or just deny me my cousin for no good reason?"

"I have a good reason. I promised Zane I would take care of her while he's away. She has an early morning and if she sees you she's not going to sleep. Right now she knows what happened, but she's not *seeing* it. Seeing it is different, and I don't want her to see you while you are like this. It'll freak her out."

"I'm sorry, I was *attacked* tonight. I killed a man. I want to see my cousin. I'm sorry if my looks aren't up to your standards, but I *did* shower. Sorry that I didn't exactly have time to reapply my makeup."

"Lia, look in the mirror." I just glare at him. "Look in the damn mirror." he growls. In a huff, I pull the shade down and flip open the mirror. *Oh.* I cleared the blood off, but I'm sickly pale. I realize my hand is shaking when I bring it up to my cheek. "You've been through hell tonight. If I take you to Mara, she's going to want to ask you a thousand questions. She's strong and brave, but she worries. You'll have to relive all of this and *you* don't need that. Not tonight. You need rest and time to deal with this on your own. I'm helping you both, even if you think I'm being an ass."

"You are," I shut the mirror. "You are being an ass. But you're right. I'll call her really quick, just to let her know." I let out a breath before I hit her name and listen to the ringing.

"Lia, is Enzo there?" I hear her worry and put a smile on my face, hoping she can hear it.

"He's here and being bossy. The crew is here, and he's taking me to crash at his place for the night. I'm fine, just ready for bed. I just wanted to let you know that all is well and being dealt with. Thanks for your help."

"Of course." She sighs deeply. "I'm so sorry this happened, Lia. We will take care of this."

"Hey, my night was pretty dull until then, so there's that. Just," I take a breath, "don't tell Aren."

"Why aren't we telling your brother?" Enzo butts in when I hang up. He's going far over the speed limit, so I look down at my hands. He seems at ease, but if I pay too much attention to the world flashing past us, I'll be sick. I hate cars. I have my driver's license but I never drive. Getting my license had been hard enough. I'd nearly had a panic attack multiple times when I had to drive with the instructor. To this day, I'm pretty sure I only passed because Aren pulled some strings. The last time I thought I'd take myself to the store, I sat behind the wheel until my butt went numb, then I got out of the car and went back inside. "Lia?" He looks at me when I don't answer.

"Can you just pay attention to the road?" I snap. "I survived an attack tonight, it would be a shame if I died because you wrapped us around a tree."

"I won't fucking crash."

"Sure, that's what everyone says until they *die in a car accident.*"

"Shit." Enzo noticeably slows the car, probably remembering how my parents died.

"We aren't telling Aren because my step-brother will freak the fuck out. He'll rip the town apart if he finds out something happened to me."

"Doesn't sound so bad. Maybe he'll help us find out who is behind all these attacks lately."

"Sure, doesn't sound bad to *you*. He's already my shadow, I can only imagine him if he finds out I snuck out to go out with some friends and got attacked."

"You saved yourself."

I just sigh and let the conversation fall aside. Sure, I saved myself. Because he wasn't there. Because I didn't listen and stay put until he got back. I shouldn't have had to save myself. He should have been there. He'll blame himself for it right until he gets pissy that I went out without a harem of bodyguards.

"Just keep your mouth shut."

"Not something I'm known for. Plus, how are you going to explain leaving the hotel and staying with me?"

"I'll just tell him you kidnapped me and watch as he beats the shit out of you. Maybe you'll be less annoying in a coma."

2

ENZO

Lia sleeps through most of the day. I have cameras set up throughout my house but most of the rooms are usually turned off. They're installed as insurance in case someone untrustworthy finds themselves in my company. At lunch, I turn the camera to her room on. I watch her sleep, curled up on the bed, her mouth hanging slightly open. Seeing a usually perfectly put together woman sleeping with some drool sliding out of her mouth makes me feel horny as hell. That she fought for her life the night before makes me want to tear the world apart. That man's death should have been drawn out over days. She'd been too kind in her kill. A kill she never should have needed to make. I text plans to Zane on and off through the day. The men behind these attacks need to be stopped. It's one thing for them to go after our men, men who've made the choice to live in this life, and all that it entails. They are well compensated and we will take care of their families if anything happens to them. It's something else to go after one of our women.

Zane was pissed to hear about the attack against Lia. As one of the few people that showed his wife kindness during her very turbulent life, Zane's almost as protective over her as he is over Mara. I can only imagine how her step-brother would react to the knowledge. I'm surprised he agreed to the trip with Zane in the first place. I've only known them for a year, but this is the first time I've seen Lia without her brother pressed to her side. I can understand his overprotectiveness. Their parents were killed in a car accident and I'm sure their uncle would have taken control if Aren hadn't immediately stepped up and made his position clear. If he'd given an inch regarding his sister, she probably would have been sold off to the highest bidder before her parents were cold in their graves.

I get work done while my house guest sleeps. In the last year we've directed most of our energy to bringing the Papazian and Moretti family together. Even with Aren's help it took us months to comb through all of the legal and illegal projects the Papazian family was involved in. We are still going through all of their people and working to replace those not happy with the new leadership. I can't remember the last time I got a full night of sleep. Zane and Mara had to move quickly to take their crowns and bring their families together. Clearly, even now, we still have plenty of people that are unhappy with the change. It's been an ongoing issue, having little rebellions pop up, and we've lost a few men due to the annoyances. But this is different. Seeing Lia standing over a dead body, knowing she'd been in danger, sends anger spreading through me like wildfire.

She stirs while I'm on a call with Romano about ramping up guards at all our businesses. The last thing I want is someone that works for us being kidnapped or murdered while walking to their car at the end of a shift. I watch her on the camera as she looks around slowly and then reaches for her hair. She stands and stretches before wandering around the room. She finds the door to the bathroom, and I shut off the camera. I finish my call and head to the kitchen to ask that lunch get started. It's an hour before Lia finally makes her way from the guest room to find me. She looks like a different person than she did the night before. Her makeup is perfect, her clothes are what I'm used to seeing her in, and her smile is fixed on her lips like nothing strange happened the night before.

"Good morning." She greets me.

"Good *afternoon*, Sunshine." I quirk a brow at her and watch her frown before she checks her phone.

"Ah," she shrugs. "Fine, I'll take it back. I hope you had a terrible morning. I'm sure you did since you didn't have my company." Lia nudges a shoulder into me and I just shake my head.

"Lunch is in the dining room." She falls in step behind me, the click of her heels sounding against the hardwood. "Why are you wearing those?"

"You're wearing your shoes, so clearly you don't have a problem with shoes inside."

"Yes, but mine are comfortable." They actually aren't the best, but they aren't fucking heels, so I still think I win this argument.

"I'm comfortable in heels. I wear them all the time. I'm so comfortable in fact, that I killed someone in heels just last night. Is that all," I turn back in time to see her waving her hands around, "cleaned up?"

"It's been dealt with."

"Then those people earned every penny they made. Because, ew."

"Ew?" I step into the dining room and move to the side so she can get through the doorway.

"Yeah, *ew*. Blood is gross. I think I got some in my nose because I can still smell it."

I hand Lia a plate and pile some food onto my own. My chef is no Maria, but I can't pull her away from Zane, no matter how often I've tried. He does okay though, and he also makes a potent drink. "I'm just going to leave that alone." I shake my head. "I spoke with Zane-"

"I'm sorry, you did *what*?"

I speak slower this time. "I spoke with Zane. You know, head honcho, married to your cousin? Tells really bad jokes?"

"First of all, he's only *half* head honcho, thank you very much. Mara is the other, prettier, and *better* half. In fact, I don't think they are 50/50, anyway. I think it's more of an 80/20 situation, with Mara in the lead."

I stare at her, doing everything I can to not grin in encouragement. She just matches my stare with her steely gaze. "Was there a second point, or was that it?" I finally ask as she takes a bite of roasted vegetables.

"Oh, yeah, what the hell? I thought you weren't going to tell Aren?"

"I didn't... I told Zane."

"Yes, Zane, who is currently with Aren."

"And Zane, who can keep his mouth shut. I've protected your secret from you brother-"

"*Step-brother.*" She interrupts, an edge to her tone.

"Anyway, Zane has ordered you to stay here with me until they return. He'll tell Aren the hotel you were staying in was compromised and that I gallantly agreed to keep an eye on you until your overbearing *step*-brother can take over in his guard duties."

"I'm sorry, he *ordered* me? I don't take orders from him. I take them from the *actual* head honcho, Mara. Why can't I just go stay with her now that I don't look like death?"

"Because after her meeting today, Mara is going to meet Zane to finish their work together. He doesn't want her left unattended right now, and he wants to jump into finding out who is behind all the attacks."

Lia lets out a puff of air to show her displeasure before stabbing a poor piece of broccoli and shoving it in her mouth. I take a moment to pull my eyes away from her lips. "I'll take you over there once you're done eating so you can see her before she leaves. Zane wants me to make sure only our assigned guards are with her and that they are prepared to be extra vigilant."

"It's sweet how much he loves her."

"It's gross. I'd take breathing in the scent of blood all night over having to watch them make out one more damn time."

"Aww, you're jealous of their cuteness." There is a lightness to her grin that I don't think I've ever seen before. She's always sharp edges when I see her. She jabs at me with quips, she is a protective shield with Mara, and she's a cold statue around Aren.

This is a new Lia and I wonder who else gets to see her like this. Does everyone know this part of her exists? Is this what lays under the masks she's always wearing? Or is this just another mask?

"Lia, you do not want to know the things I've witnessed with those two, okay? The amount of meals that have been ruined..." I make myself cringe even though I am far too happy for the two of them. Even if they never invite me back to their bed. Too bad that was only a one and done situation.

"Okay, roomie, any house rules I should know?"

3

Lia

I hate to say it, but Enzo was correct. Mara spends our entire visit going between clucking at me like a mother hen and raging against the world that this is still happening a year after her takeover. I haven't seen her kill anyone, but I know she has. I also know that she's at least been in the room for every execution to go down since she and Zane came to power. They agreed to run our family together, and they've done so every step of the way. Today though, was the first time I really saw the killer in Mara. There has always been a fire blazing in her gaze. Anger towards her father and her refusal to go down the aisle without a fight. But this is a new side to her. One that would relish having her shoes and clothes soaked with blood. Again, ew. I'm usually the one to throw myself at her, squeeze her a little too hard in a hug, and stand as a feral cat against anyone that looks at her wrong. Too many years have gone by seeing her hurt. Those tables have turned and now she's feral, pacing circles around the courtyard while Ani runs underfoot.

"Mara, you have to leave soon to meet your husband," Enzo states dryly, arms crossed as he leans against the doorway to the kitchen. He spent his last hour flirting with Maria, who only answered him in curses, telling him to leave her and her book alone.

Mara glares at him, murder glinting in her gaze.

"Unless you've decided he just can't scratch your itch. My offer to whisk you away still stands." He flashes a wink and Mara swings back her arm and chucks Ani's ball straight for his groin. He dodges at the last second, the ball bouncing off this thigh and flying. Ani barks and gives chase while Enzo gapes at her. "Not nice, Mara. I'll have to tell your husband you're being a bad girl."

Mara sways towards him while I just watch all of her demons come out to play. She actually reaches up a finger to *boop* his nose. "Don't tease me with a good time, Enzo. You know my husband does his job well. If he hears I nearly broke your dick, I'll just spend all night being rewarded."

"He *would* reward you for that, the prick." Enzo chuckles before he pulls her into a tight hug and kisses the top of her head. "Still my favorite brat. Travel safe." He returns her nose boop and I think I maybe *did* die last night and woke up in some alternate reality. Mara breaks away from him before she gives me a squeeze. Enzo and I both give Ani some love before Enzo walks her to the SUV and checks in once more with her small army of men. We wave her off and then he turns to me with a wide grin. "This is when we throw a huge party right? Mom and Dad are out of town; that means we invite everyone we know to their house?"

"I mean sure, if you want to die. You *are* a grown man with a house of your own. It would be possible to throw a party there."

"Nah, that doesn't sound fun at all." He holds out his elbow for me and I wrap my arm through it like it's the most natural thing in the world. I've walked like this with Aren at countless events. Enzo doesn't hold me in a possessive way as we walk, though. There is always a sense of possession with Aren. I push those thoughts away as Enzo opens the door to his car for me. His hand lingers at the small of my back as I climb in, and then his warmth is gone and the door shuts. My phone dings, so I dig it out from my purse already knowing who it is. I checked in with my friends this morning to make sure all of them got home safe and felt guilty for not thinking to check last night after everything happened. Since I know it's not any of them, and I just saw Mara, it only leaves my step-brother.

A - You're with Enzo?

L - Hello to you, too.

A - ...

A- Zane told me you're now staying with Enzo and Mara is coming here. What happened? He says nothing, but clearly something is going on. Are you okay?

L - I'm fine. I think there was another attack or attempted attack and they are all on edge. Just being safe.

The lie sits heavy in my stomach. I may have been the one to tell everyone to keep Aren out of this, but *I killed someone* and he doesn't know about it and that feels wrong.

"Everything okay?" Enzo looks at me as he starts the car and waits for the gate to open.

A - Call me if you need me. I can come back if you need to get away from Enzo. Or I can bring you here with Mara.

I respond to both men that I'm okay and then sit back in my seat. "It's not a house party at Mom and Dad's house, but how about you take me dancing?" Clearly, I learned nothing from last night.

"Didn't you kill a man last time you went dancing?"

"Yeah, but I'm sure that won't be a regular occurrence. I mean, what are the odds?" I grin at him, daring him to make poor choices with me. His gaze is dark when he looks back at me.

"Around here? Seems pretty likely. But a little trouble can be fun."

"A little trouble? If I'm going to get into trouble, I hope that it's big." I grin at him, unable to resist.

"Wow, I didn't know you had dick jokes. I can arrange for us to go out in a few hours; is that good?"

We go back to his house and I explore for a bit while Enzo makes some calls. I'm just starting to get bored being nosey when he tells me he'll be ready in an hour. I take my time finding a sexy, short, white dress. Luckily, I always pack to be prepared for every occasion. I re-do my make-up to make it more fitting for a night at the club, giving myself more of a shadowed eye and dark red lips. I'm adding some curls to my hair when he knocks at the bedroom door. I turn off the curling iron and unplug it before I call him in.

"You ready?" He steps in, and my mouth goes dry. *Oh*. I've always found Enzo attractive, it's hard not to. But I'm used to seeing him in perfectly tailored suits or, occasionally, workout clothes. Now he's standing there with dark slacks and a tight fitting button down with the sleeves rolled up over his forearms and a few buttons left loose at his neck. His hair is still a little damp, like he just jumped out of a shower and the scent of his cologne is a mixture of citrus and spice like a deep bergamot. His pupils are blown wide when our gazes meet and I realize that while I was taking in the sight of him, he was doing the same to me. "Looks like you're missing shoes." He says after a hard swallow.

I grin, feeling wicked from the feel of his attraction. It's nice to be wanted openly, and hardly ever happens when Aren is around. No one would dare cross him to appreciate all the work I put into my appearance. I pick up the high heels I sat on the small desk in the room he gave me. The heels are high with straps that wrap up past my ankles.

"Let me." Enzo sits on the chair and pats his knee for me to put my foot there. Heat rushes through me like wildfire. He knows exactly what he's doing, the dark promise in his gaze tells me that. Attraction morphs into *want* for this man. Everything about him right now is calling to me in a way I haven't let myself feel in quite some time. I lift my foot and he holds it in his large hand, his fingers going right to the arch of my foot, massaging there for a moment before he slips the shoe over my foot. Then he rests it on his chest while he works the strings up my leg, twisting them with ease before tying it off. His fingers trace over my skin as he goes, and he lingers at the back of my knee for a breath more than necessary before he gently places my foot down and slowly lifts my other. He gives it the same attention, a quick massage, lingering touches. This time he pauses for longer before he places a kiss just above my knee. A dark promise that starts an ache at my center. Once he puts my second foot down, he leans back in the chair, draping an arm over the back of it to give himself a look of ease. I see past that though. His muscles are tight and his gaze is hungry as he looks me over much slower this time.

"You can have all the fun you want tonight, but you are my responsibility. Stay close, and you *only* come home with *me*. Understood?"

I narrow my gaze at him. The heat he just fanned against my skin dissipates with his words. I arch a brow and give a large, fake smile. I'm so tired of being told what I can and can't do. I'm tired of being a *responsibility*. I thought he was seeing me as more. As an *attractive woman*. Hopefully, one that he wants to fuck. Instead, I'm the class pet he has to care for until the teacher gets back. Fuck that. "You got it." I promise while making it my one goal to drive him up a wall tonight.

4

Enzo

I messed up. I'm not sure when I made the mistake, but a mistake was clearly made. The entire ride to the club passes in silence but I am highly attuned to the constant tapping of one perfectly manicured finger against Lia's smooth thigh. We had a moment back in her room, but then she pulled away. It's still throwing me to see her without her bodyguard of a brother hovering nearby. There's always been a quiet tension between the two of them. A possession in one another that doesn't quite ring as sibling affection. They aren't blood, and they were older teens when their parents got married. Both are attractive, it certainly wouldn't surprise me if there was or had been something else between them at some point. I glance at Lia and think back on all the times I've seen them together. She's always held herself back with Aren. She gives affection freely to Mara and even Zane but I can't remember ever seeing her give Aren affection in the same way. Aren is the same. He has a quiet affection towards Mara, but there is definitely something different in the way he acts towards Lia.

I could be very off base. They dealt with loss and then had to band together as a united front to stay safe. I can certainly understand that. Zane and I had to be a similar united front when his family was killed. We grew up together and already had a bond, but it took a stronger hold when it felt like it was just the two of us against the rest of the world.

"So, should I text Aren your location? Make sure he knows where you are and what you're up to?"

Her finger stills for only a moment before it taps again. She doesn't look at me. What the fuck did I do to piss her off? I debated having my driver bring us, but the idea of trusting anyone else to drive while Lia was in the car seemed like a terrible choice. Right now, she's mine to protect and no one can do it as well as I can. I know she needs a safe way to let off some steam, so I can give her that tonight, even if she's pissed at me.

I pull up in front of one of our clubs. I've kept up with visiting Papazian territory on a regular rotation, but on a night with Lia, I'm only going to go to Moretti turf. Our world has been dangerous enough lately, and after she ended her night covered in blood only yesterday, I want tonight to be different for her. Even mad at me, she knows how this goes. She sits in the car until I come around to open her door. Both legs swing out together and she takes my hand as she stands. I pass the keys to the valet and we step into the club together with only a nod to the bouncer.

The music is pulsing, loud enough that I feel it in my ribs. The lights are dim with a purple glow and the bar makes an L across two walls. There are standing tables and a second story with private seating to overlook the dance floor. "What's your drink?" I lean in, my lips brushing against her ear. I feel her small tremor and fight back a grin.

"An Aviation cocktail." She gives me a soft grin before flipping her hair over her other shoulder and leaving me as she gets lost in the fray of dancing bodies. I get to the bar and place our orders and frown when I'm handed her drink. Of course she'd get some pretty lavender looking thing. She's easy to find in the crush of bodies. She dances with abandon, her body moving to the music like she's creating it with her hips. Fuck. Men and women swarm her. She's surrounded, but she looks at ease so I stand back and just watch the show she's so kindly putting on. When the song ends, she opens her eyes and sees me. She takes the drink, eyes it carefully, and then drinks deeply. Her lipstick doesn't even smear on the glass. She finishes it and then hands it back to me. I raise a brow. "You could take your time with it."

"No, thanks." She shoos me away with a fan of her hand. "You told me I can have all the fun that I want. So fetch me another." She turns her back on me and goes back to dancing. A man joins her, and she leans back to press her back to his front. She closes her eyes when his hands land on her hips, and I finally catch up to the game at hand. I acted protectively and pissed her off. She's going to play by my rules, but she's going to toe the line all night. Instead of getting her another drink, I leave her glass at a table and sip on my own while I watch her. It's fun seeing this side of her, and her streak of rebellion is turning me the fuck on. She might be trying to make me jealous, to prove some point with me, but she doesn't know that I love sharing. Watching my woman with another man has always been my favorite kink. Not that she's my woman. But she's certainly acting like a brat that needs some special attention right now. I watch the man's hands move up and down her body and admire how she keeps control of the situation, forcing him to follow her lead in the dance. Not that he's doing much more than grinding against her for his own pleasure. When the man's lips fall on her bare shoulder, her eyes open and instantly find mine again.

She has to read the hunger in my gaze. Every cell in my body wants her. I want to take her right here. To stand in front of her and push her dress up so I can find her wet center. I want to make the man at her back brace her so I can fuck her hard to the pounding music. She licks her lips, and a silent battle of wills passes between us. We both want the other, but it feels like a forbidden line to cross, and neither of us moves to step over it. Instead, Lia raises her arms and rests her hands at the back of the man's head. She pushes his mouth harder against her smooth skin. His fingers make fists against the material of her dress before they slide down to the short hem. Lia doesn't break her stare with me as his fingers move her dress up until

I can see a flash of black lace at her center. She moves so that her legs are spread apart just enough for him to put his leg between hers. He turns her to face him and puts his thigh right back between her legs, moving her so that her feet barely touch the floor and she depends on her center staying on his thigh. His hands go to her ass and I don't miss the way her hips follow his pull as she rides his leg. He leans forward to kiss her, but she turns her head, giving him her neck instead. She looks back at me again and I move through the crowd so that I'm in her view again. Lia is enjoying her little game, and while she's getting hot and wet, I can't stop thinking that part of my rules for the night was for her to go home with *me*.

My cock is hard and pressing against my zipper in desperation as I watch her hold his shoulders and use him. He drops her back to her feet before she gets close. He leans down to say something in her ear, probably trying to whisk her away to the bathroom, or if he has the cash, he could take her to the private seating upstairs. Both things would be within the parameters I left her with, but whatever he asks has her giving a small shake of her head. I take that as my sign to step in.

"Got your drink." I thrust my glass into her hand as I step in front of her, forcing her boy toy to take a step back.

"Dude, what the-" I turn and his words cut off when he sees me. Anyone that comes in this club with any kind of frequency knows me well, and this man must recognize me with the way his mouth snaps shut.

"Thanks for the show. I think I'll take it from here though." I give his shoulder a pat before I reach forward to adjust Lia's dress and wrap my arm around her hips. With a quick nod he backs away without argument and Lia's head whips around so she can glare at me.

I lean down to brush my mouth against her cheek before whispering, "I like how you play the game."

"I wasn't aware we were playing a game." She lifts my glass to her lips and takes a hearty sip from my drink. Guess her drinks don't have to be a pretty color.

I just grin at her. "Let's not lie to one another-"

A shout rings out near the front door, and then the world shakes with a small explosion. The sound of my glass crashing against the floor as Lia drops it to grab my arms sounds louder than any of the screams that break out. I move on instinct, turning my back towards where the blast came from, blocking her with my body. Chaos erupts around us.

"Enzo!" Lia shouts but I just pull her tight against my body with one arm as my other goes to my gun. Fire blazes at the main entrance and as everyone rushes past us towards other exits; I see bodies where the blast went off. Everyone moving makes it hard to see if the attacker is still there or if they threw something in and then rushed past the building. Someone bumps into my shoulder as they run past, desperate for an escape.

"Fuck!" Keeping a tight hold on Lia, I move us through the distressed crowd, going to a side door that's marked for employees only. I open it and push her inside first, taking an extra moment to scan the building. The fire is moving quickly, eating up the walls and licking at the spilled alcohol. I join her in the darkness before I take her hand and drag her behind me towards the employee exit. If I didn't have her with me, I'd make sure our people got out safely. I'd clear the building, but right now, all I can think about is Lia. She's in danger *again* and I need to get her out of here.

I push the heavy door open and we walk out into the cool night. The smell of thick smoke clogs my lungs. I tuck Lia under my arm, pressing her face to my chest as I move us down the back alley and then across the street to move away from the building and the crowd of people filtering into the night. We move two blocks over with rushing feet before I stop and press her against a building. I cover her with my body as I finally release her so that I can pull out my phone. The text with our location and a demand for an immediate pick up goes out with a few quick strokes against the phone screen. "Lia, are you okay?" I tilt her head up with a single finger and find her eyes wide and glassy. As my adrenaline slows I realize she's shaking from head to toe, staring over my shoulder at the cloud of smoke rising above the buildings. "Lia!" I say harsher this time, drawing her gaze to me. She's going into shock, but I'm not sure if she got injured, or if it's just shock from what happened.

"Are you hurt?" It's not really a question but more of a demand.

Her lip trembles but then she takes in a deep breath and shakes her head. It's not enough. There's a new desperation sitting heavy on my chest as I watch her hold on to reality with nothing more than a fingernail.

"I need the words, Lia. Are you hurt?"

Her hands reach out and squeeze my arms, and she seems to pull strength from that hold. "No, I'm not hurt."

5

AREN

Zane's phone rings while we sit around a large table heavy with food. I'm bored as fuck and want any excuse to leave this meeting that won't end. He needs to secure allies; he needs to play nice, but after days of playing the delicate game of kissing ass and laying down the law, I'm worn down to the bone. I hoped Mara showing up would signal an end to this mess, but it just continues. More people popped up for us to meet when word got out that Mara was here. We have three more days of meetings laid out before us and I just want to go home. Not having Lia at my side is like missing a fucking limb and it makes me antsy to not see her and know that she's out of harm's way.

Zane signals that he's taking the call and leaves the table so I plaster on my smile and enter the conversation again, not really knowing what I'm saying. Mara laughs and the sound of it draws a smile out of me despite myself. I can count on one hand the amount of times I've heard her laugh in all our lives before she met Zane. In the last year I've lost count of her joy. Despite the non-stop danger around us, she's carved out a life for herself in this dark world and she doesn't hold back in living it to the fullest.

Zane stands between me and Mara and rests his hands on the back of both of our chairs. "Sorry, I'm going to have to cut this meeting short. I've already dealt with the bill though, I appreciate all of you taking the time to join us this evening." Zane offers his hand to Mara and I wait for her to stand before I follow suit, protecting her back as Zane tucks her against him. He doesn't wait for anyone to draw him into an explanation. The king and queen have spoken, and now they make their exit. None of us say anything until the limo pulls up to collect us and all three of us are tucked inside. The stiffness in Mara's spine releases as we gain privacy and she turns on her husband. "What happened?"

He doesn't look at her when he answers; he looks directly at me when he says one of his clubs was attacked. "There were some casualties, and the building is lost."

"Is it connected to the string of attacks lately?" I ask, assuming it must be, but it's a clear escalation.

"We don't know the culprit yet, but Enzo is going to send me access to the video feed. It seems likely it's all connected, though." He pauses, giving his wife a quick glance before his attention goes back to me. "Enzo was there with Lia. They got out safely-"

His words continue; I can see his mouth moving, but I can't hear anything over the ringing that starts in my ears. Lia.

"Aren!" My head jerks up and I find Zane and Mara frowning at me. "She's okay. She wasn't harmed."

I slam my fist into the door of the limo and the flare of pain in my knuckles is enough to clear the haze. "Why the fuck was she there in the first place? She shouldn't be out in clubs. Especially not with some asshole like Enzo. I told you I didn't want her there with him! I told you she should have come with Mara-"

"Aren!" Mara's voice has a bite to it. "Lia can go out and have a bit of fun! She's an adult and you hardly let her out of your sight. You and Enzo are our most trusted, if she couldn't be here with you, he is the only other we trust to keep her safe."

"And why exactly couldn't she come with you, Mara? Why were you whisked here while she was left behind?"

"You'll watch your tone with my wife." Zane warns.

"My cousin can hold her own." I snarl back, anger becoming a fourth being in our limo.

"I came in order to help close up these meetings. We need everyone to fall in line right now while we have these insurgents causing chaos on the home front. Zane thought he and I meeting as a united front would help to end questions that remain about how our family is going to run from now on. Lia didn't need to join us for that. Zane said she's fine, so you can be angry that she was in danger, but know that Enzo made sure she was safe and he is not the enemy here. We need to find the real enemy, and end them before this goes on any farther."

I stretch out my aching fingers. "So what, we are stuck here to finish these meetings before we go home?"

"I'll move them all up so we can still meet with everyone but get out of here." Zane offers, his fingers already flying over his phone as he makes it happen.

I pull out my phone, but Mara lays a hand over mine. "Just let her rest for tonight. It's already late, and it sounds like she had a busy night." I nod but I still send her a message.

A - Tell me you are safe.

I don't get a response until we are back at the hotel. My knee bounced violently the entire ride, but the ding of a notification has everything in me stilling as I open my screen.

L - I'm safe. Going to bed.

6

Lia

I wake up with a pounding headache, curled on a sofa with a soft blanket covering me. I remember Aren texting me while we were still in the back of the SUV that picked us up. I recognized the driver, but I couldn't place his name; I was just thankful the face was one that I knew after everything that happened. After we were picked up, Enzo had the driver take us around the block a few times slowly. He searched quietly out the window as we passed the chaos over and over. I just stared at my fingers, refusing to look out the window. The men talked quietly, but I didn't hear them. Enzo made a call, and then my phone dinged. I was surprised Aren didn't actually call me, but maybe he wasn't at a place where he could. Maybe he didn't really care. Maybe he was just annoyed that I got myself into trouble and now there was a mess to clean up. He doesn't even know half of it.

I finally responded to Aren when we started back towards Enzo's house, and then Enzo's attention turned to me. He didn't say anything, or if he did, I didn't hear him, but his gaze stayed on me. He took my hand in his and his thumb rubbed my pulse point for the rest of the ride. I showered, trying to rid myself of the scent of smoke, and changed into another comfortable pair of sleep clothes while I threw out another dress. Two for two. Maybe Aren was right in keeping me locked away all these years. Clearly, going out is not for me.

I stretch and sit up. I can't quite remember how I ended up on the sofa. I showered and changed in a haze the night before, and I don't know why I wouldn't have collapsed on my bed.

"Hello, Sunshine." Enzo sits at ease on a chair across from me. His laptop is balanced on his leg, which is crossed over his knee while he lounges back like one of his buildings wasn't blown up last night while we were inside it.

"I fold." I say as I sit up. I want to worry about the state of my hair, but I just don't have it in me. I don't have an ounce of energy to spare, and I feel like I'm on the verge of crying.

"Oh? Is this a hidden talent of some sort that you want me to be aware of?"

"I give up. I rebelled twice and almost died twice. The universe is telling me to stay in line, so that's what I'm doing from now on." I feel like a petulant child as I cross my arms and lean back against the sofa. Enzo just laughs at my pain, which makes me bristle. Any of the heat that I thought was between us last night is gone as my insides go cold against the world. It hits me suddenly. I miss Aren. Our relationship has been on the toxic side since our parents died, but it has always been off. I had a crush on him from the moment we first met, which was awkward to deal with as a teen thrown into the same house as him. I spent years pushing those feelings down and doing everything to hide any signs of them. Most of the time, I even forget they exist. Like right now. Right now I just want him here as my brother. As the one that has protected me again and again and used his own body as a shield against me and the world. I don't feel safe without him at my side.

"Do you want to talk about it?" Enzo's voice is oddly tender.

"How did I get on the sofa?" I ask instead.

He debates for a moment before he closes his laptop and leans forward. "You wandered in here half asleep and said you couldn't sleep. We turned on a movie and you drifted off on the sofa a few minutes later. I didn't want to move you."

"Did you drug me? Why don't I have any memory of this?"

"Stress." He offers un-helpfully. "So, is Aren rushing home to sweep you into his arms?"

The way he says it makes my hair stand on end. "What's that supposed to mean?"

"You tell me."

I stand and fold up the blanket before brushing my fingers through my hair. "Is there any food around here?"

"Lia. Sit down." Enzo's demand is like a hand at my throat. He leaves no room for me to deny him. So I sit and clutch the blanket back on my lap. I hug it like a pillow, while I use it like a shield. I feel like he can see right through me, and that pisses me off. All these years and no one has ever questioned me and Aren. "I can do the math. You were both at very sexual ages, attractive, and thrown into a house together. I mean... I'm going to be disappointed if you tell me nothing ever happened."

"Nothing ever happened." I bite out.

"Okay, see," he points to his face, "disappointed. But you certainly wanted it to, didn't you?"

"Enzo, seriously. What the actual fuck? Aren is my brother."

His grin is maniacal. "If you didn't notice last night, I'm very open-minded. And Aren is your step-brother as you always feel the need to correct when his name comes up. Tell daddy your dirty little secret. Come on, no one else is here. If something happened, I can understand keeping it secret all these years. I mean, your family wasn't exactly a fun place to be. And even this last year has been littered with issues, as you well know after your few days of hell. You didn't have a safe place to be open about what was happening-"

"Nothing. Happened." Instead of arguing or spewing more truth seeking missiles at me, he pulls out the dirtiest trick in the book. He just sits back and shuts his damn perfect mouth. He's going to fight me with knowing silence. And fuck him, but it works. "I had a crush on him, okay? But he never felt the same, and that was when I was a kid. Nothing happened, nothing ever will, and he sees me as his sister, always has, and always will. What exactly is your game, Enzo? The way you were looking at me last night certainly made me think you either wanted to watch me fuck a stranger, or you wanted to do the fucking. You weren't exactly giving off the vibes that you wanted to throw me at Aren."

"Oh, I'd love to check either or both boxes. We could do it on the same night. Would you rather that I watch first and then show you the right way to get fucked? Or do you want to start your evening on a high note, riding my dick?"

"You're sick. Can I eat now, or do you want to hear about a crush I had on a book character? Oh, I had the hots for my gym teacher once in high school, too. The arm muscles really got to me." I bat my eyelashes at him slowly, trying to push away the heat that rises at his words. There is no reason the idea of him taking turns using me should be a turn on. But last night, dancing with another man while he ate up the show... I was one second away from combustion before the jerk had pulled away to ask to whisk me to his apartment. The idea of being with the random guy without Enzo watching held zero interest for me.

"I'll go get you food; you can sit and relax. You had a busy few days." Enzo stands but strides over to me, all the confidence of a well-hung billionaire. He leans over, bracing his arms on either side of me. "But tonight, while you're laying alone in your bed and you can't sleep, think of being between me and Aren. Imagine our hands worshiping your body and making you come until you lose count and the pleasure hurts from being too good." His lips brush against my skin with his heated promises, but he leaves me with my dignity when he doesn't look at the state he puts me in. Instead, he turns to head to the kitchen and doesn't look back.

7

ENZO

Lia has been with me for days and my hand is cramping from all the self care I've been doing. I wish she kept to herself. Instead, Lia walks into a room, glowing like a ray of sunshine, and makes sure I know she's there. Her presence is now like a sunburn, living on my skin, stretching me to my limit, and creating an itch that I just can't scratch. She doesn't wear lounge clothes other than to sleep. Instead, she walks around all day wearing short dresses that tease and hug her body. Even the click-clack of her damn heels turns me on. I know any second she's going to turn a corner and appear like a fucking wet dream. It also seems Lia lost all of her normal lounge clothes. The longer shirts and leggings are a thing of the past. Now, I catch her getting water before bed in shorts that show off the bottom of her ass cheeks and a thin top that sits above her belly button (pierced by the way), and shows off the chill of her two perfect nipples (not pierced, as far as I can tell).

This is payback for my comment about sharing her with Aren. The woman is pure evil, and that just makes me like her even more. Zane, Mara, and Aren are due back any day and I'm not sure if I'm ready to be rid of her, or if I'm going to beg her to stay. For the last year, Aren has mostly kept Lia tucked away at their house. He's been the face of the family for the Papazian side while Mara keeps residence here with Zane. He and Lia aren't constant fixtures. Is he going to get back from this trip and whisk Lia away before I ever get the chance to enjoy everything she keeps putting on display?

I'm imagining fucking her with her legs on my shoulders, wearing nothing but those damn heels when I hear her coming down the hall. Her makeup is perfect as always, and the circles that persisted after the club have finally vanished. I hope that means she's getting better sleep and not that she's just gotten a better concealer, or whatever it is she uses. I drink her in, not hiding any of my attraction as she smiles brightly at me. I had trouble ignoring her before whenever we shared space, but after this torture of rooming together, I don't think I'll ever be able to not notice when she's near. Zane is going to owe me big time for being absent for so long.

"Good morning." She's too damn perky grinning at me like she isn't slowly torturing me to death. When we find the people behind these attacks, I'm just sending her in with a tight dress to take them all out. She'll do it with a smile as long as I promise to clean up all the blood afterwards. Her smile turns to a small frown. "What are you thinking about right now?"

"What?"

"You have a look of murder about you. Did something happen?"

"Oh." I straighten and adjust my tie as I do. I checked out two of the businesses closest to me this morning before she was up to make sure there weren't any issues. "I was just wondering how much you would enjoy taking out our enemies if I promised to always handle the cleanup."

"Wow, what an offer. I can't say I've heard that one before."

"I like to stand out." There is an ease between us I only share with Zane and Mara. We can banter and dance around each other like we were born to be in the other's orbit. But the pull towards her is so much stronger; maybe we are finally about to spin out of control and collide. "Speaking of offers, how many times have you fantasized about me and Aren? You know, I love sharing. I'm sure when Aren gets back we could get him on board."

All that beautiful color in her cheeks fades. I actually worry she might faint. "If you tell Aren about a crush I had years ago, I'll do my own cleanup just to have the satisfaction of ending you."

"Such violence. Let's see, that level of violence..." I count on my fingers. "Four times? Do you have a toy tucked away in that bag of yours, or do you have to settle for your fingers? I have batteries tucked away in my office if any particular toys need a little extra pep."

"I hate you."

She tries to move past me but I block her. "I think the problem is that you don't. You want me. And I'm right here. I'm all yours. We can play alone, or with a friend. Or step-brother. Like I said, very open-minded."

I expect her to push me away, throw something at me, or just walk around me. Instead, she bites her lip. Her eyes leave mine and settle on my chest. "Did you ever consider that maybe I don't want you?"

I step into her space until our chests press together. "Not even once."

"Of course not. Everyone must want you, right?"

"I'm sure there's someone out there that doesn't, I just haven't found them yet." Her eyes land on my lips. I can feel her gaze almost as strongly as if she put her mouth there. I slowly reach out to trace my thumb against her plump bottom lip. "But if you aren't ready to admit it," I drop my hand, "I won't be the one to rush you." I step around her and leave her to her breakfast while I head to my office to do a check-in with Zane. Once I'm alone, I give myself a moment to get over the effect this woman has on me before I call my friend.

"Staying out of trouble?" Mara answers.

"Never." I quickly respond. I will always be highly amused by how *little Mara* wrapped Zane around her finger in a matter of one interaction. To this day, I'm still surprised he shared her with me for a night. It was clearly all for her, to give her some sense of freedom and control, which was sorely needed, but his possessiveness over his wife is impressive.

"Are you taking care of my cousin?"

"Not in the way I'd like to."

"Enzo!" Her reaction causes her dog Ani to bark, and the sound is harsh over the phone. I hold it away until Mara tells her to calm down. "You leave my cousin alone."

"Why, you jealous?" Her deep sigh makes me laugh. "You make this too easy. Unlike your cousin. But, if she ever gives in to my charm, I'm certainly not promising to leave her alone. So you'll just have to deal with it."

"That's fine; you're out of time anyway. We are heading back tonight. Zane is having his ear talked off in the other room, but whenever they are finally done, we are heading out. Aren is staying with us tonight, but he'll probably be there for Lia in the morning."

"Aww, Daddy has to come home and ruin all my fun."

"Ew... just... I'm going to have Zane punch you in the face when we get back. You deserve it and he'll jump at the chance; he won't even ask questions."

"Mara, what happened to our love?"

"Zane's dick was more impressive, sorry." She giggles before she's interrupted by Zane.

"What about my dick?" I hear him take the phone. "Who is talking to my wife about my dick?"

"I don't really see what's so impressive about it, personally."

"Of course it's Enzo."

"What kind of greeting is that?" I lean against my desk, completely unbothered by the grumble in Zane's voice.

"You know, if any other man was talking to my wife about dicks, I'd cut theirs off, right?"

"Yeah, but I know I'm safe. If your wifey wants to spice things up, I'm the only one you trust to call. Gotta make sure my dick is still intact."

"Actually, I don't think you need it."

"Lia might think differently."

The silence that greets me is deafening. Then, I make out harsh whispering and realize Zane must have covered the phone to talk to Mara. I let out a sigh of my own while I wait. They really make it far too easy to screw with them. "We'll deal with all this tomorrow. I want a meeting in the morning to discuss everything that happened here and everything that's been going on. I want to take time to visit the club site, if you can swing it."

"You got it, boss!"

The phone goes dead as he hangs up on me without so much as a goodbye. Prick.

8

AREN

Staying the night with Zane and Mara makes my skin itch. The house is plenty big enough, and it's late when we get back, but knowing that I'm close to Lia, yet I have to wait to see her, keeps me up most of the night. I've heard from her, but with everything going on, I feel the need to see her alive and well with my own eyes. She's my responsibility. I'm all she has, so it will always fall on my shoulders to protect her. It's not a job I would ever turn away from, but I feel the weight of it while I'm away. It doesn't help that I left her alone, and she somehow ended up staying with Enzo, and then she was in a club when it was attacked.

I'm downstairs pacing the moment the light from dawn shines through my window. I'm not sure when Enzo is supposed to bring Lia, but I won't feel good again until I see that she's safe. I want to whisk her back home, but I know Zane wants to speak to all of us about everything that's been happening. Whatever prompted Mara to come to Zane and Lia to stay with Enzo, had Mara pissed off. I know they will not end this meeting today until there is a solid plan in place to push back at the threat. And we should. We stood aside for too long with Mara's father. He pulled the family into darker deals than any of us ever wanted a part in. Hayk and Vram only brought shame to the family. Growing up in the Mafia certainly puts all of us on the wrong side of the law, but before Hayk, we were never involved with the human trade. Now with Zane and Mara in charge, they are fighting against trafficking. They've made moves to cut off dealers, and half of the people they've already taken out were men that were upset about the deal falling through. Just taking out the garbage.

I lose track of time but a guard announces someone at the gate, and I go on alert. I'm standing when Lia steps in. Her eyes find me instantly and her face breaks out in a huge grin before she runs forward to hug me. Her scent envelops me and I squeeze harder, lifting her off her feet. "Missed you, kid." I kiss the top of her head after I place her back on her feet and she returns the kiss with a shove. Something flashes in her gaze, but she shuts it down and turns her attention to Mara. She goes running again and nearly knocks Mara over as she throws herself at her. The women both squeal with laughter as they right themselves, and I can't help but join with a smile of my own. Some piece of me fits back into place now that I see her.

"All safe and sound." Enzo nudges me and I try to remember when he walked in. He eyes Lia in a way I would kill other men for. I make a fist and straighten my spine. He might be Zane's most trusted, but if he put his hands on Lia, I might just rip his face off. Zane heads towards us and I wonder if I gave away my feelings, or said my thoughts out loud. Instead, he walks right up to Enzo and punches him square in the jaw. Enzo lets out a curse, barely staying upright.

"What the fuck?" He shouts, holding his jaw and looking incredulous.

"Not sure, but Mara told me to punch you." Zane shrugs a shoulder like this is normal practice, and Enzo's eyes dart to a guilty-looking Mara.

"Told you he wouldn't even ask why."

"I'll get you an ice pack, but let's get this meeting over with so I can kick all of you out and enjoy some time with my wife." Zane leads the way into the dining room. It has become our meeting place since there is plenty of room for all of us, and his housekeeper, Maria, always fills the table with plenty to eat while we talk. This new family was built around this table, and all the tough decisions have been passed between the five of us. These meetings have made our own home feel empty when Lia and I are there. Mara has built herself a safe space, and that transfers to us while we're here. Whenever we go home, I go back to feeling like it's Lia and I against the world. For so long, it felt like that with the added pressure to free Mara from her father's grasp. She did that on her own though, but Lia and I still seem stuck in some limbo. We're part of the family, but still on our own.

I watch her sit, and frown when Enzo takes up the seat next to her. I want her to be happy; I want her to find love, but no man has ever been worthy enough. Especially not Enzo, with his smart ass mouth, and the reputation that follows him. I pull back the chair on her other side and glare at the man as I sit. Maria comes in and tuts at Enzo.

"Hello, beautiful." He grins at her, but she just pinches his cheek, making him whine in pain.

"Did you deserve it?" She asks, giving his growing bruise a pat.

"Yes." Mara answers for him; any sign of guilt is now replaced by amusement.

"Humph." Maria hands him an ice pack before leaving the room again. She returns with a little cart filled to the brim. My mouth waters as she lays out drinks and food.

"Okay," Zane draws our attention after everyone has filled their plate. "I think it's time all of us are on the same page about everything that has been going on."

Lia draws up straight. Her hand drops away from the table and goes to her lap, and I don't miss the way her eyes dart to me.

"We've secured deals with two families. Drawing everyone back into the fold has been our top priority. We secured the Derian and Bernardi's for trade and protection. They've agreed to work together and with us. But we still have to clean some house. These recent attacks on us cannot go unnoticed. Punishments need to be handed out, and quickly. Lia and Enzo are our best chance at finding out who was behind the attacks."

"What was the other attack? I know you sent Lia to Enzo because something happened, but I only know about the club." I look at my step-sister and I know she's hiding something. It wasn't some random threat that sent her to Enzo, and I will find out what happened before we leave this table. Mara glances at Lia, I notice the motion out of the corner of my eye, but I don't stop staring at her.

Lia finally lets out a breath and looks up at me. "You know there have been seemingly random attacks against our people." Lia takes a sip of her drink before continuing. "One of those idiots followed and tried to attack me."

"What?" I stand, but Zane shoots a frown in my direction and I force myself back into my seat. My heart is erratic, attempting to leap from my chest. *Attacked.*

"I'm fine, obviously. He came at me right as I got back to the hotel room we'd been staying at, but I ended up killing him with my dagger. I called Mara, and she sent Enzo and a clean-up crew to take care of everything. I stayed with Enzo. That's it. We know there have been a few of these random attacks against our people; this time it was me." She shrugs, but I'm not sure if I've even blinked since she started her story. Lia, innocent and always so put together Lia, killed a man. With a fucking dagger.

"I want to keep the two of you here for right now. I think we are stronger if we are together as one unit, but I also hope that Lia and Enzo may end up being able to help figure out who is behind all of this so we can take them out, and take them out quickly." Zane continues like I didn't just find out I almost lost Lia twice during one little trip away from her. I swear I'm never letting her out of my sight again.

"I thought you wanted to get rid of us to be alone with your wife?" Lia teases, but I watch his expression tighten.

"I was hoping you could all stay with Enzo. Your stuff is

already there from the hotel, and Enzo has plenty of space.”

“You guys really can’t just keep it in your bedroom?” Enzo asks dryly, and I have to agree. Mara shifts with reddening cheeks and that is too much for me to deal with in one sitting.

“It’s fine. If Enzo is fine with it, we’ll stay with him until we can get all of this under control. I’ll make some calls to the Papazian allies I trust the most to make sure they are monitoring everything on our end while I’m not there to follow up.”

“Sounds like a solid plan. Enzo, tomorrow do you think we could go to the club?”

“Fuck man, keep it in your pants. It’s still morning, we could head over there now-”

“That is all.” Zane stands, and his dismissal is clear. Mara is just grinning ear-to-ear, looking up at her husband, and I have to wonder if there was some little blue pill in Zane’s drink or something. Lia stands first and runs around the table to pull Mara into a hug. I just think about how everyone kept the fact that my step-sister was attacked from me. They actively lied to me. The betrayal cuts deep, but I know Lia is really the one behind the blame. She didn’t want me to know, so she pulled everyone else in to keep it from me. Our gazes meet, and I see the guilt rise to her cheeks. She twirls a finger in her hair, a nervous habit she showed me the very first time we met. My bag from the trip is right by the front door so I pick it up and fling it into Enzo’s arms as I grab Lia by the elbow and lead her from the house.

9

Lia

I know I'm in trouble. Aren's anger is like a storm cloud following me the whole car ride back to Enzo's house. Aren is silent as Enzo gives an over-the-top tour of his house and shows him to a room across from mine. I know Enzo can feel the tension, but he fills the silence like a kid that inhaled sugar instead of taking a nap. It's impressive, actually. I'm almost distracted enough to forget the attraction that's been simmering between us the last few days. I'm well aware I could have had him if I'd given him the smallest inkling that I wanted him. Something held me back from making the final move, and that opportunity is probably long gone now that Aren is here. Enzo finally excuses himself to make some calls but I stand in front of Aren's bedroom door like the good little step-sister that I am.

I push away all the dirty little thoughts Enzo put in my head. I cannot lust after Aren. Not only is he my step-brother, he's my best friend, and the only constant I've had since I was a teenager. He's been with me through thick and thin, and all of his rules have been for my protection. My few days of freedom from said rules is enough to show he wasn't exactly wrong in his thoughts.

"What the actual fuck, Lia?" He barely waits for Enzo to turn around the corner. Aren's arms cross at his chest, and he frowns at me. I feel his disappointment in my bones.

"I went out dancing. I did nothing wrong. I just lived a little."

"And you almost died!"

"No, I was attacked, and I killed the bastard that dared to come after me!" I raise my voice, my hackles rising. We've had our fair share of screaming matches, but all the guilt I felt disappears under his anger. "You don't get to tell me I'm in the wrong! I went out with some friends, I was safe, I came back to our hotel. Someone else made the choice to attack me. They could have attacked me when I stepped out to get a coffee from the damn lobby! Don't victim blame me, Aren! And. I. Killed. Him. I held my own just fine without you!" I step forward, really on a roll now. Aren's eyes are wide and his silence spurs me on. "Maybe if you ever let me have a little fun, I wouldn't have gone out the second you were away! Maybe if you'd let a man get closer to me so that I don't kill the batteries of all my damn toys, I wouldn't have felt the need to *get some* while you weren't up my ass! I missed you, I did. But I also felt like I could breathe for the first damn time in years." My voice lowers and I realize I went too far. Hurt replaces his anger in a flash.

"Aren..." I draw in a deep breath and watch as he closes himself off. His features take on the stoic look he always has when he's dealing with family business.

"No, you're right. We live in a dangerous world, and I've seen the worst of it. I've done all that I can to protect you from it, but you're an adult. So go on and find someone to fuck. I have some numbers I can give you. Men that I've kept at bay thinking I was protecting you."

"I don't think I'll have to go that far." Years of pent-up feelings for Aren come spewing out in a thinly veiled effort to make him jealous. I want Enzo and I wonder if he'll drag me right off to his room if I tell him so. But I also want the man standing in front of me. I've wanted him for so many years the feelings are tangled up in everything else that we are. I look at him and remember the pain I felt when I knew he was off with some other woman while he kept every male away from me with the threat of death. I look at him and see the man that comforted me all the times I woke up missing my mother, woke up scared of the violence that surrounds us. I want

Aren. But I don't know how to tell him.

Something flickers in Aren's gaze and a shock of electricity passes between us as his eyes flick to my lips. Has he ever done that before? Then he moves forward, grabs me and spins us until my back is pressed against the wall next to his door. "You want to run off and play with Enzo? You think he has what it takes to please you? I'm sure some of the men I've scared away could offer you more." His words are a violent growl. He pounds a fist on the wall beside me, making me jump. The energy coming off of him in waves is confusing, and I don't know what he's giving off and what I've put out there on my own.

"Maybe I'll take their numbers. Enzo likes to share, maybe I'll have myself a little party." I cock a grin before I shove at Aren's chest. I know he moves back on his own, that he's strong enough to keep me pinned against the wall if he really wants to. I turn my back on him, my heart racing. It takes everything in me to saunter away from him, swaying my hips the way I've been doing to tease men since puberty.

"Fuck!" His word is a growl followed up by the sound of his fist hitting the wall again. I don't pause. I laid out a dare for myself, and I'm about to follow through with it. The sizzling attraction between me and Enzo is calling like a siren. If it pushes Aren over some edge I'm not even sure exists? Even better.

Enzo is leaning against the wall right as I turn the corner. He raises a single brow at me, full of judgment and amusement.

"Listening in on conversations you weren't invited to?"

"Yep." He grins. "Though, I feel like I had a little part in that conversation. Man, those naughty thoughts of yours are really starting to brew over, aren't they? You really gave it to him and he's only been here for, what? All of five minutes?"

I pop a hip and give him a grin. "Maybe I'm just tired of waiting for something to happen. Maybe I want to be the one to make the moves for once."

"I respect that. So, Sunshine, what moves are you making? I'll happily play the pawn to the queen. Move me as you will. Want to play?"

I feel his promise. I remember how he complimented me after I killed my attacker. Enzo helped ground me after the chaos of that night. He protected me and got me out of the club when my body shut down against the surprise of the explosion and fire. He watched over me to make sure I was okay. He wants me.

"Yes." I whisper the word but my body burns with the single syllable. His grin is feral, a dangerous promise for what my evening will hold.

"Tell me, Sunshine." His voice lowers as he whispers against my ear. "Do you also want Aren?"

Icy fear hits me in the chest, but I push it away. Enzo is a safe space. I can trust him. I do trust him. I swallow past a truth I've always held close to my heart. One that he saw right away. "Yes. I want you both. But that'll never-"

He places a finger against my lip and forces my gaze to meet his. "Tonight, you don't worry about anything. Tonight, I want you to trust me and just feel what you feel. Can you do that for me?" I nod, but feeling a little bratty, I dart my tongue out to lick at the finger he still has over my lips. A shadow comes over his gaze as he pushes his finger into my mouth. I close my lips over it and suck hard. "This is going to be fun. Yellow if I'm pushing you too far. Red if you want to stop. Got it?" I suck again before biting down on his finger. He pulls his finger from my mouth and swipes it over my lips before he pulls me against him and devours my mouth. All the pent-up tension between us flames up and burns my skin as he takes what he wants from me. His hand twists in my hair, tugging my head back until he has me where he wants me. I moan against his mouth, and he just uses that as an excuse to taste deeper, his tongue dancing with mine before he sucks on my bottom lip.

I melt against him. I haven't been with anyone in years. Now I'm burning up in need, the throb between my legs is instant and almost painful. "Please." I beg against him, pressing my body closer like a cat in heat. His other hand wanders over my body before cupping my ass and drawing me against him. I remember dancing at the club, riding a stranger's leg while Enzo watched me. I would have gone farther on that dance floor with this man watching me. Now it's him I'm tasting, his warmth surrounding me.

"Please what, Sunshine?"

"I need you so bad." I cling to him, not liking that he pulled back to ask me what I want. I wonder if Aren ran off to his room. I wonder if he even cares that I came after Enzo. I wonder if Enzo would be pissed if he knew I was thinking of Aren.

"Babe, we are just getting started. Have you ever come so much you cried? Because I think you'd cry so beautifully for me ."

"Enzo! It's been so long... Please."

"What a needy girl." He leans forward and sucks at the sensitive spot on my neck. I moan louder than I mean to, my body arching against him. He picks me up, his hands cupping my ass and my legs go around him. My arms twine behind his neck and I pull him back into a kiss, hoping he'll carry me off to his room and finally end my suffering.

10

Enzo

"You aren't taking my sister anywhere." Aren is standing in the hall as I turn the corner, Lia braced in my arms, her legs wrapped around me.

"Aren-" Lia's hand falls from my shoulder. Her lips are swollen and red from us making out. I can still taste her and feel the smoothness of her skin against my hands. Her hair is mused and her dress askew. I can't wait to finish stripping away all her layers. The tension between them is a whole other entity in the room, though. I've been watching them, watching Aren and how he watches his step-sister. Always watching her. It goes beyond over-protective and enters obsession territory. I know it well, Zane looks at his woman in a similar way.

"It's too late, Aren. I'm taking her to my room. She's a grown woman, and she's very interested in going with me. Do you want to make sure she wants it?" I lower her until her heels touch the ground. Then I turn her to face him, pressing her back against my front. She leans to rest against my chest automatically. My hand goes to her thigh, inching up slowly until she's arching against me. She's pliant and needy, rubbing against me like a cat.

"Take your hands off her." Aren's gaze is crazed.

"Why? Do you want the honor? Maybe you want to put your hands between her legs and feel how wet I've made her?" I reach the thin lace covering my prize and make sure her dress is pulled high enough for Aren to see everything I'm doing.

"Enzo," my name is a whisper on Lia's lips, a quiet beg for more. She has zero concerns about her step-brother watching what we are doing, in fact, her body is clearly very into it.

"Have you ever touched her there? All these years, being so close. Together all the time and keeping all the other men away from her. Surely you've wondered how she feels." I slip my hand under the lace, my fingers reaching her wet pussy. My teasing falls away, forgotten as I get my first feel of her. I groan against her shoulder as I sink my fingers against her soaked skin. Fuck.

Aren's angry gaze falls from my face, which he clearly wants to punch, to where my hand has disappeared. My fingers dip into her, sliding right in from how wet she is. The sound she makes is a spark in the air. A pulse of darkness that invades all of us. "Haven't you ever wondered how she tastes?" I free my hand, bringing my fingers to my mouth and sucking them, drinking her in and moaning at the flavor of her. "Fuck, Sunshine, I can't wait to get my tongue in you." I let her dress fall and grip her hips, pulling her back so she can feel what she's done to me. I don't think Aren has blinked. I'm not sure he's even breathing. I grab her hand and drag her around Aren towards my room. Aren follows us, his feet stomping to the same rhythm as my pounding heart. I'm not at all surprised when he follows us right into my room.

"Sit in the fucking chair, Aren. Watch as I make your sister scream." I nod to the chair just inside my room before I pull Lia back to me so I can take her lips again. She moans against me, and the rest of the world falls away. She tastes so good, and when her hands wrap around me, her fingers pulling at my hair, I'm lost. I pick her up and her legs go around me again, like she was born to cling to me. I forget about her brother for a time as I lay her on the bed, shoving her dress up her legs and take in the little triangle of lace I've been playing with.

"Take them off." I order, taking in the blush on her cheeks and the mess of her hair spread out on my pillow. On my fucking bed. She doesn't hesitate, but reaches down to slide the lace off, and at the last second her eyes dart to Aren, who did in fact, sit diligently on the chair in my room. She uses her foot to flick them at him. Her grin is a taunt and my hunger for her grows. "Spread your legs for me, Sunshine. Show me." I glance behind and find Aren staring at our little show, his step-sister's underwear held tight in his fist, his knuckles white. "Show us what we're missing."

Her confidence fades for only a moment. She bites her lip and her eyes dart between us, but then she inches her legs apart, slowly revealing her pussy, shining with need. "Aren, my man. I'm about to eat her out like I haven't eaten in years. Look at that perfection."

"Shut the fuck up." He growls the order, which I happily ignore.

"You're right, I'm wasting time." I crawl onto the bed with her, fitting my body between her legs before pulling them so they rest over my shoulders. And then I devour. Nails scrape against my scalp as I dive right in, none of that slow build-up shit. No, I want her screaming, and I want it now. It doesn't take long as I suck on her clit and stretch her with my fingers. She tries to buck against me but my free hand pushes down on her pelvis, holding her right where I want her. I take and take until she's shaking under me. Her hands pull at my hair and then she pulses against my fingers, exploding around me, yelling out my name. I lap at her, letting her fill my mouth and groan against her. "What a beautiful mess you've made, Lia." I lift my soaked fingers to her mouth, and she takes what I give her, sucking hard and swirling her tongue over the tips of my fingers. "Such a good girl, coming so hard for me."

"Enzo, god." She releases my fingers and her head falls back to the pillow as she struggles to catch her breath. Little tremors still run through her, but I'm nowhere near done with her yet. I turn to Aren and make a show of licking my lips. I hold his gaze for a moment, watching the storm he's fighting. He wants her so badly, but he makes no move.

"Take off your dress, Sunshine." I order, not breaking Aren's gaze. Daring him, daring him to get up and join her on the bed. He glares at me, refusing to look even as Lia moves behind me to get her dress off. She tosses that at Aren too. She nails him right in the face and I can't hold back my snort of amusement. "Someone is being a very good girl, following all my directions, while also being a complete brat. You must bring that side out in her." I grin. "I like it. Does it look like I'm taking good care of your little step-sister right now? You think you can do better?"

He says nothing, but he's strung so tight I feel the urge to poke him just to see if he'll break. "Not going to take what you want?" I question. "Then enjoy watching as I take it. I'll just keep her screaming only my name. If you can't join us, then why don't you take out your dick and take care of yourself before you bust something." I send a pointed look toward his straining cock, pressing against the zipper of his slacks. Then I go back to the woman on the bed, the one both of us want, but the one I'm taking.

11

LIA

Holy fuck, what am I doing? Enzo prowls toward me. He's a fucking predator on the hunt and I'm his next meal. It's so easy to follow his orders, to let him take charge even though I'm always fighting for my own say. Now look at me, still shaking from the mind blowing orgasm, with my step-brother watching from a chair against the wall. I can't believe he actually followed us in here, actually sat down and watched what Enzo did to me. And I can see the hunger there, hunger for me. I've had a crush on him since the first day we met, but I've sensed no returned feelings from him. Not until Enzo used me as a tempting piece of candy to dangle before his eyes. And he'd looked. I've never been so turned on in my life. I'm aching to be filled, to have skin on skin. Enzo grips my ankle and pulls me down the bed, grinning when I yelp.

"Don't you dare hurt her." The words are a growled order from Aren, but I can't look at him, not when Enzo looks like he's about to swallow me whole. I'm on fire with need, and he sees it. He's ready to deliver.

His smirk is a wicked promise. His words send a little thrill through me when he calls back, "No promises. But if I do, she'll like it." Then he rips his shirt off, showing off the intricate tattoo I noticed once before, but from much farther away. His muscles are defined and make my fingers itch to trace them. We've been dancing around this for days with all the teasing and flirting, and now he's here and mine. Then I think of Aren sitting in the room with us. He's been a wall I've had to climb over when all I've ever really wanted was to curl in his arms, to have him as mine. He's not, yet he's here. Watching. Enzo doesn't seem to mind, in fact he's just been taunting him since all of this started. He knows I want Aren, and he's doing all he can to push my step-brother over the edge. Enzo wants me, but I know some part of him also wants to watch me with Aren. He wants to share me. He's taunting Aren to come and touch me, to join us on the bed. This is a dangerous man I've found myself with, and that fact has my heart racing as his fingers find my center again. He goes slower as he enters me with three fingers, curling them deep inside me.

"So tight for me. Has Aren been keeping all your fun away?" I nod my answer. "I'll make it all better. You let him hear as you scream my name again. I still want to see you cry so beautifully for me. I wonder how many times you'll have to come before you do?" He keeps moving his fingers in and out of me, curling them deep inside as his thumb brushes over my clit. I reach out to cling to his arms. I'm not sure if I'm trying to pull him closer or push him away. He keeps moving just under the pace that I need. He's keeping me right on the edge making no moves to slow or speed up.

"Enzo..." I want more. I start to worry his hand is going to cramp, or he'll get tired. I can feel another orgasm just out of reach, and I want it to be mine so bad that I lift my hips, urging him to give it to me.

"Look at me, Lia." His thumb presses harder against my clit with his order, and I respond instantly. My eyes flash open and meet his gaze. "Such a good girl. I'll give you what you need, don't you worry. I want you to look at Aren for me."

I hold Enzo's gaze for a moment longer, a little afraid to look at where Aren is sitting. I can't believe that I threw my panties and dress at him. What came over me? Something snaps in place when his gaze meets mine. His legs are spread wide, my clothes still clenched tight in his fists. He's leaning back against the chair, every inch of him rigid and still. "Does he have his cock out? Is he getting himself off while watching you?"

"No." I whisper. I can see Aren's cock straining against his pants, but his hands are nowhere near it. His jaw ticks at my answer but Enzo doesn't even slow his pussy teasing.

"Aren, I'm going to edge her like you're edging yourself. I will not let her come again until you take your cock out or leave this room. She's so close too. I can feel her pussy fluttering, begging for me to give her what she needs. Tell him, Lia. Tell him how much you need it." His fingers curl inside me again, drawing a pitiful moan from me as he eases his thumb away from my clit, refusing to give me the stimulation I so desperately need.

"Please. I need to come again. Please." I've never been this desperate in my life.

"Fuck you, Enzo." Aren frowns, but his gaze darts between me and Enzo.

"Please. Please let me come." I cry out again as Enzo continues his assault against me. He's playing me so well, pacing himself perfectly to keep me right at the edge. My whole body is shaking, and I taste blood. I realize it's because I bit the inside of my cheek. "Enzo, please!" I beg again.

"It's not up to me. It's Aren's move now. He can get up and leave this room and I'll make you come all over my fingers again. Or he can take out his cock and jerk off to the sounds of you coming."

"Fuck!" Aren actually sounds desperate as he stands. My heart drops a little as I think he's about to walk out. But his eyes don't leave mine as he unbuttons his pants and pulls the zipper down. My pussy clenches around Enzo's fingers as I watch Aren pull his pants and boxers down before taking up his seat again, large, heavy cock in hand. "Stop teasing her, Enzo." Aren's order sets Enzo off and he grins at me before his hand does something magical and I combust around him. I scream Enzo's name and my body lifts off the bed as I come for the second time tonight.

"That's two, and I haven't even had my cock in you yet." Enzo's mouth hushes my cry. I cling to him, needing his warmth and comfort as I try to piece myself together again. "Are you okay?" He asks quietly, so that only I can hear. He brushes a finger over my cheek with a tenderness that makes my heart swell. He shouldn't be able to taunt Aren, make me come like he did, and then be this tender with me. His gentleness helps all my little pieces come back together again. His gentle kiss to the tip of my nose makes me giggle and fills my chest with a lightness that threatens to make me float away. "Are you ready for more, or do you want to pause? We don't have to do anything else tonight if you don't want to; we can stop here. I think I've brought you some pleasure to get you through the night." He winks, but his hand also wanders to my breast and flicks at my nipple.

"You haven't made me cry yet." My eyes dart to Aren. His hand grips the base of his cock in a way that looks like it might hurt. He's not moving his hand, but it looks like if he does, he might come right then and there. I want him to. I want him to come to the vision of me.

"Mission accepted." Enzo reaches for the nightstand and pulls out a condom. He rips the wrapper open before handing the condom to me. "Put it on for me, Sunshine?" I nod and take it. Before I put it on for him though, I lean forward and kiss the tip of his cock. He stills and I feel the need to do a little teasing of my own. Enzo has been in control for too long this evening, and it's time to put him down a peg. Maybe it's been a while since I've done this, but I'm no stranger to porn, and I have good instincts. I circle my tongue over his tip before I take Enzo into my mouth. He's rock hard as he rubs against the roof of my mouth. I take him deep but avoid the back of my throat out of fear before I suck on him. His hand comes to my jaw, and he rubs there in gentle encouragement. I look up at him and he's staring unblinking at the sight of me taking his cock deep in my mouth. When I suck again and take him a little deeper, he groans and his eyes snap shut, his head dropping back.

I bring my hand to his base and start to draw back, sliding my hand up him, but he reaches out and grabs my wrist. "Save it for another night, Lia. Fuck, you are too good. I want to be inside you though. I need to stretch that pussy so you only ever fit me perfectly."

"If you say so." I give the tip of him one more long, teasing lick before I sit back and slide the condom over him slowly.

"You're okay?" He checks in again. When I tell him yes, he draws me forward to kiss me slowly like we have all the time in the world. His hand plays over my nipple again, sending a new electric sensation through me. "I want you to ride me, but I want you to look at Aren. Do you think you can do that?"

"What?" I glance worriedly at Aren again. Enzo has been talking low for my ears only.

"Until Aren decides to join us, this is the only way I can give you the both of us. And you deserve to have everything you want. So I'm going to do what I can to give it to you, okay?"

"Enzo-"

"Trust me?"

I nod my answer, and he lays down on the bed before pulling me so that I can straddle him backwards. I feel awkward until his hands smooth over my ass and he lets out a groan of pleasure. He settles my center over him but doesn't try to penetrate me yet. Instead, he bends his legs so that I can hold on to his knees and he slides me over his long, hard cock. I go loose as he draws out my pleasure. "Open your eyes, Lia." I wasn't even aware I closed them, and I have no idea how Enzo knew I closed them, but I open them at his command and find Aren watching me with a pained expression.

"Ready for me, Sunshine?"

"Yes, please." I answer Enzo, but I eye Aren's cock as I do. His hand still has a death grip on his base, but I want him to move his hand and stroke himself to me. I want to taste him like I just did to Enzo. I want him to take his turn once Enzo is done. I don't know if he sees all that want on my face, but Aren slowly moves his hand up his cock as Enzo moves under me and moves the head of his cock to my center. My head falls back as I lift to hover over him. We move together slowly so that I can slide down on him, taking him deeper, inch by inch.

"So good," I whisper as he stretches me in the most delicious way, filling me in a way my toys never can. I sink all the way down on him and feel him pressing against me from the inside.

"You see how well your sister takes me?" Enzo asks over my shoulder, directing his question to Aren. Aren doesn't bother to answer, but his gaze is on my pussy, his view showing him just how Enzo is filling me. His hand moves again slowly as his gaze moves farther up to take in the sight of my breasts before he meets my gaze. The moment his eyes connect with mine, Enzo moves us, lifting me and drawing me back down to ride him. My breasts bounce with the movement, but I'm so overwhelmed by Aren's attention and the feel of Enzo's hands on me and his cock filling me that I can't be bothered to care.

12

AREN

Fuck. Fuck. What the fuck? One minute I'm arguing with Lia about the dangerous situation she put herself in, and the next I'm trailing after Enzo as he runs off with my step-sister. How did I end up in this room with them? And now I'm so close to coming I can barely skate my hand over my cock in fear of making a mess of myself. Lia. *My Lia* is riding another man's cock and taking it so well. But I know she can take more, I know she can do better. I want to taunt her and tell her to ride him harder. I want to demand she take me in her mouth and take me all the way to the back of her throat. Enzo isn't pushing her enough, but I don't dare open my mouth. I don't know what kind of game Enzo is playing, but he played it well and dragged me right along with him. There's no way I could have walked out of the room when he was edging her, drawing me deeper into his plan.

I watch Lia's breasts bounce as she rides Enzo's cock. She's holding on to his legs for support as she lifts her body to draw him out almost to the tip, before falling back on him to take him so deep inside her she groans each time. The sounds she's making... I wanted to rip his head off when she came and called out his name. Even as she looked at me, she called *his* name as he fingered her. He's tasted her, now he's inside her, while all I've done is watch and try not to come. All these years of keeping everyone away from her, laying my silent claim on her, knowing it was never a claim I could make a move on, and he sweeps in and takes her.

"God, yes!" She cries as he grabs her hips and moves her in a new way. A way that makes her feel even better than she did before. He's finding all these spots, all the ways to make her scream for him. The jealousy that rises from my center is one that could spell out his death if she wasn't between us. Instead, something inside me snaps. Any control I was pretending to have tonight is gone. I stand and stride over to the bed, my hand gripping my cock in a desperate plea not to come yet. Lia's gaze widens and something changes in her at my approach. There was some part she was holding back that she finally hands over. I watch the change as she moves with greater ease, riding him harder and begging me to come closer. She reaches out a hand towards me, and when I take it, she tugs me forward.

Even as she rides Enzo, she looks at me with a silent question. Then her gaze goes to my cock, and her hand reaches out tentatively. She doesn't touch my cock, but places her hand gently over my death grip. I feel her question, and I finally hand myself over to her. I release my cock and grab her wrist instead. She's so delicate under my grip. Someone I've tried to protect for so many years. Now I'm about to strip her down to the barest instinct. There will be no coming back from this.

I throw all my fucks into the wind and step onto the bed before I place her hand on my cock. I move even closer until my cock is right in front of her face. "Show me what you can do." I order before I grip her hair and tug her face forward. Her moan is loud and vibrates over my dick as her mouth closes over me. I feel the change in how she rides Enzo. More desperate as she chases her own finish and takes my cock right to the back of her throat without hesitation. My words were like a dare for her, and she's going to show me what I've been missing all these years.

"Fuck, yes." Enzo cries from under her.

"You will not come yet." I order. He's been messing with me

this whole fucking time, he can force himself to hold back until I've come all down Lia's throat.

"Not a fucking chance." Enzo agrees, his hands moving Lia's hips in a circle over his cock. She cries out again but sucks me down harder before drawing her head back to truly mouth fuck me. She dances so perfectly, keeping up with Enzo while using her hand and mouth to draw me right to the edge. I reach out and slap the side of her breast, watching how her eyes widen in surprise and pleasure. Then I reach down and rub her clit. I can feel Enzo too, but I ignore his dick and focus on the feel of her clit rolling between my fingers as she bounces on his cock. Her tongue dances over me, and I finally let myself loose. I grip the back of her head and draw her forward until I feel the back of her throat, then I let all the built-up tension finally release. I moan her name as my come fills her mouth, and she swallows around me, taking everything I give her. Then I swirl my fingers over her clit again and she comes on Enzo's cock, falling forward into my arms as she pulses around Enzo.

His gaze flicks to me, and I give the smallest nod of permission. He responds by slapping her ass and grabbing her hips again to lift her and crash her back down over his cock. She moans at the sensation as he does it a few more times before he finally lets himself go over the edge and fills the condom stuffed inside her. Lia's whole body is shaking as she clings to me. I lift her chin and see the fresh tears shining on her cheeks. The tears Enzo was determined to get her to shed. I lift her off him and turn her so he can see. He did work hard for this after all. He sits up and reaches out to her, his thumbs brushing away each and every one.

"So beautiful." Then he scoots to the edge of the bed and reaches out to take Lia from me. She's still weak and shaky. I know her body is right at the edge after everything that happened tonight. He draws her against his chest before looking me dead in the eye and motioning for me to take up the other side of the bed. "You know as well as I do she needs both of us right now. We just put her through the ringer."

Lia agrees with a small pouting sound. I roll my eyes, but

push the covers down and crawl in beside her. She's laying on his chest but I reach out and trace her bare back slowly. I linger at the curve of her hips and watch as she melts under the attention. Enzo removes his condom and ties it off before tossing it into a small trash can on the other side of his nightstand. Then he kisses her forehead softly and closes his eyes like this is the most natural thing in the world. Lia follows him in sleep. I keep my hand on her and wonder what the fuck I just did.

13

LIA

"Lia, do you want to go with me and Zane to the club?" Enzo stands over the stove with bacon sizzling in a pan. I woke up to a man on either side of me this morning and panicked. The memory of last night is like a haze. A fever dream from lack of male-given orgasms over the years. But it was hard to deny what happened last night when I woke up with Enzo's chest under my cheek and Aren's arm wrapped around my waist.

"Um, I think I'll just stay here. I don't exactly have the best memories of that club." I sit at the table and watch him flip the bacon with ease.

"Oh, come on, it wasn't all bad." He shoots me a wink and I try not to spiral. Aren grumbled that he had to shower the moment he woke up and pulled himself out of the bed without so much as a second glance in my direction. I had his dick in my mouth the night before and that's not going to just go away. If he regrets it, he's going to have to tell me because avoiding me isn't much of an option. Shit. "Lia." My name is an order on Enzo's lips and I straighten to attention. He woke up this morning and kissed me. He covered my cheeks in kisses before slowly tasting my lips; morning breath be damned. We showered together and, even though he was a gentleman in the shower, he was sure to touch every inch of my body. He massaged tense areas and teased sensitive spots. He washed my hair and massaged my scalp until I moaned as loudly as I had while taking his cock. But we didn't talk. Not about the night before or what all of this means.

"Lia." He calls and I realize I got lost again. "Just feel what you're feeling. I've got you, okay?" His words are a gentle promise and I drink them in. "You guys can talk today while I'm out of the house. Let him know how you're feeling and give him space to come to terms with what happened, okay?"

"How-"

"You're pretty easy to read, and last night was a lot for anyone. With the history and pent up," he waves a hand in my direction, "everything, it's a lot to work through. But you two have to talk to work through it." He puts a plate down in front of me, filled with freshly cut fruit, eggs, and bacon. "Just remember, I'm not going anywhere, okay?"

"What if I don't actually want you?"

"Again, you're a terrible liar. You want us both, and as far as I'm concerned, you can have whatever you want. " He leans in and kisses me, taking it just deep enough to make my toes curl before he pulls away. "You text or call me if you need me. I'll abandon Zane on the side of the road if you need me to come back, okay?"

"I'll tell him you said that."

"I'll say it to his face. Now, are you going to talk to Aren, and call me if you need me?"

"Sure, Dad."

"We both know Aren is the one with the bossy daddy kink."

"What?" I nearly choke on my bite of bacon.

"Oh, come on! He wants to spank you for misbehaving just as much as he wants to fuck you. I would bet money that he would get a hard on just from you pouting and calling him Daddy."

"Go away now." I take another bite in an attempt to cut off this conversation before I combust. Enzo, of course, reads me and grins in triumph.

"See you, Sunshine!"

Aren is hiding from me. There is no other possible explanation for why he hasn't come out of his room. I ate, cleaned up the kitchen, and wandered the house waiting for him to appear. Then I got worried that I missed him and wandered the house again to make sure he wasn't sitting somewhere I'd already been. Now I sit on the edge of my bed with my door wide open so that I can stare at his closed door. He's hiding from me like a coward. The longer I stare, the madder I get.

I lean down and undo one of my heels and chuck it across the hall and into his door. It thuds gently, but the sound isn't quite good enough, so I take off my other heel and throw that one harder. My anger rises to a point I feel like steam might come out of my ears like in some old school cartoon. I grab my purse and fling that too. I'm already holding my pillow to toss when his door finally opens. I throw the pillow anyway and watch with mild satisfaction as it smacks Aren right in the face. He staggers back out of surprise before he looks at the mess laying in front of his bedroom door. Then he looks at me with a small frown.

"You know, you could knock like a normal person."

"Sorry, I thought we were acting like children. That's why you've been hiding all morning isn't it?"

"Clearly I wasn't hiding. You knew where I was or you wouldn't be throwing your wardrobe at my door. Unless you just have something against this door?"

"Are we not going to talk about what happened? Are you just going to hide until I trip and hit my head and forget all about it?"

"Is that an option?" He deadpans, though I catch the small tilt at the corner of his lips.

"No. It's not. I'm as graceful as a fucking ballerina, that'll never happen." I cross my arms and make no move to cross my room. He can come to me. "Enzo went to meet with Zane. If you want to talk, now is probably the best time." I try to shroud myself in layers of protection. He's going to tell me this was all a mistake and that he doesn't think of me that way, he was just caught up in the moment. Enzo told me to tell Aren my feelings. He said to just lay it out there for him, but now that Aren is standing across the hall from me, I'm not sure that I can. Aren pushes his fingers through his hair and looks at me with an odd expression. He almost looks like he's been caught doing something naughty... and I guess he's not wrong. "Aren..." I sigh his name, trying to push past all the feelings welling up.

"Last night was my fault, okay? If you regret it, I understand, and we can go back to how things were. Enzo... I told him I was attracted to you. And Enzo is, well, a bit of an instigator. I know he pushed your buttons to get you to follow us to his room, and both of us messed with you to get you to join. We played dirty, and it wasn't fair. I should have talked to you before anything happened; I was just scared. I still am. I don't want to lose-" My words cut off as he crosses to me in a few long strides.

"Lia." His arms come around me and pull me against his chest. "You'll never lose me. Last night was not your fault. Nothing was wrong with what happened, okay?"

My heart stutters, and I freeze against him. "What?" He keeps a tight hold on me so that I can't look up at him, but I can feel his heart pounding away in his chest.

"Lia, I don't regret last night, but it's not going to happen again. Our world is dangerous; it always has been, and..." He sighs and I can feel his struggle. But I have struggles of my own. I'm doing my best to blink back my tears before he sees them. "I can let my guard down around you. I can be at ease with you. But if you were mine... If you think I'm overprotective of you now, just know that I'm taking it easy on you. We did nothing wrong last night, and all I want is for you to be happy, but I can't let something like that happen again."

I jerk out of his arms. I'm close to losing any control I have left, and I don't want him to feel bad for making his decision. If he sees me cry, though, I know it will hurt him. "I understand." I whisper, biting my lip to push away some of my emotions. "Even though you say it's okay, I am sorry about last night. It shouldn't have happened that way and I should have made sure we were on the same page first. I just got caught up in everything. But," Enzo told me to tell him my truth, so I will, even if it kills me. "I want you to know that I've always been yours. You've always been more than a step-brother to me. And I only felt safe enough for everything that happened last night because you were there. You've always been my safe place, and that won't change. But I've also wanted you for years and I won't pretend that last night was just a fling for me. I'm attracted to Enzo and I'm interested in him. There's been something between us, and I want to see where that leads. But I'm not going to deny that I have feelings for you, too."

Aren looks shattered for one second before all emotion on his face disappears behind a mask. "I think you should see what happens with Enzo. And if he does anything you don't like, you tell me so that I can kill him. Now," he drops his hands away from me and steps back, putting space between us and letting my words crash to the floor between us. "I have some calls to make. I need to make sure everything back home is going well while we aren't there to oversee it."

I swallow hard and then force a nod. "Do you need me to reach out to anyone? I don't have anything to do today, I can help." He tells me no and then escapes back to his room, shutting the door behind him and ignoring all the things I threw at his door. I don't move to pick up my mess. Instead, I collapse on the edge of my bed and swallow back the tears that are threatening. He doesn't want me. Maybe there's some attraction there that he got carried away with last night, but I'm not someone he wants to pursue. I breathe in his words and breathe out my disappointment. I don't know what this means for my relationship with Enzo either. Does he only want me if he can share me with others? Am I willing to be with someone else? I don't know. At the club I had fun with the stranger knowing that Enzo was watching me, but last night there had been so much more, and I'm not sure that's something I can have unless it's with Enzo and Aren.

My phone rings so I drag myself to my nightstand. Big Cock shows up on my screen along with a new picture of Enzo's face. That ass stole my phone at some point and changed his contact info.

"Really?" Is all I say when I answer. Enzo just chuckles in response.

"What? I wanted to make sure you knew it was me." My amusement fades a bit. The sound of his teasing hits differently after my conversation with Aren. The pain of rejection swells suddenly and there's no fighting it off. It's like being hit in the face with a brick. I let out a pitiful sob, and the line goes silent. All of it is too overwhelming. "Sunshine, what happened?" His tone turns sharper, serious, as he hears me breaking.

I stand and rush to my door, pushing it shut before Aren hears me. Now that I've started to cry I can't get it under control. I feel stupid over the whole thing, but I also feel like my heart is breaking. "Lia? Please talk to me. This is killing me. If you don't answer me I'm going to turn on the camera in your room and spy on you to figure out what's wrong."

That cuts through some of my pain. "Excuse me?"

"My entire house has cameras. Most of them I keep off for the privacy of my guests, but I can turn them on whenever I want. Now tell me what's wrong."

I can hear the tremor that's still in my voice when I answer. "Well, *now* I'm worried about being watched. Where the fuck is the camera in my room? Have you turned it on without me knowing before? Oh my god, do you have last night recorded-"

"Lia, no, of course not. Unless you're into that shit? I can record it next time if you want-"

"No!"

"Fine. I've only turned your room camera on once since you've been here. It was just the first night you stayed with me and it was only because you slept in so late that I worried about you. I turned it on to make sure you were okay and I turned it off when you woke up. I'm very respectful, thank you very much. Now please tell me what's hurt you." There's a short pause. "Did you talk to Aren?"

My sigh is probably answer enough. "He doesn't want me."

"Bullshit."

"Enzo... I... do you still want me if it's just you and me? I know you like to watch and share, but I don't know that I have it in me to be shared with anyone else but Aren." The tears start again. "But I really like you and I don't want to lose you too. I just don't know if I can be with someone I don't have feelings for-"

"I'm coming home right now." There's a gravelly edge to his voice now.

"No, finish with Zane. I'm fine, I just," I let out a small breath, annoyed with how pitiful I sound. "I need to know if you still want me?"

"Shit, Lia. Of course I still want you. I'm leaving now; I'll be home in twenty and we'll talk about this in person, okay? I don't want to talk to you like this, not when you're hurting. But I want you, far more than I have any right to. I'll be there soon. Do you want to stay on the phone with me?"

"Enzo, I'm not a child. I'm okay. I'll see you when you get back."

14

Enzo

"I have to go." I announce to Zane the moment I hang up with Lia. Shit. I messed this up. I pushed them both too far, and they weren't ready for it. Now Lia is hurting, and she's alone. Lia's doubting herself and no one is there reassuring her. She's fucking perfect, and I want to punch Aren in the face for making her think anything less. She loves him, and I know she wants me, but she's not in love with me, not yet at least. But she loves Aren, and he just broke her by telling her he doesn't want her. Not only that, but he fucking lied to her, because I know damn well he wants her. I knew that before he let her suck him off last night.

"Is everything okay?" Zane asks. We spent the last hour walking through what's left of the club and the surrounding area. He noted a few places with cameras and sent some muscle to the businesses to get copies of the tapes from the night of the attack. Normally police would have done that already, but our men on the inside are letting us take charge so we can hand out our own justice.

"Yes, just a," I pause and look away from him, "complication." I don't know that I want to tell him what is going on between Lia and I and her feelings for Aren. That seems like a secret for her to reveal.

"Anything I can do to help?"

"No, I just need to go home." I give him a one-finger salute as I leave, but my jest is half-hearted. I get home and nod towards the two guards I put in place since Lia has been staying with me. The house is silent when I enter. It hasn't been silent since Lia. Between her heels, her blasting music like a rebellious teenager, or talking a mile a minute, she doesn't breed silence. Both the bedroom doors are closed like a standoff between her and Aren. I eye the shoes, purse, and pillow scattered on the floor and wonder what the fuck that's about. I pick them up before I knock on her door. I want to rage when she opens the door. Her hair is pulled back and her eyes are red rimmed. But her back is straight and her emotions are tucked away, hidden behind a mask of ease that I'm sure she perfected for all her social events.

"Care to explain this?" I ask, holding up her discarded items. Her mask breaks for a moment as she glares at them.

"Nope." She pops her "p" and steps back so I can enter her space. "Care to show me where the hidden camera is?"

"Nope." I pop my own "p" and grin.

She pouts and steps into my space. Sadly, the stuff in my arms keeps her from getting closer. "What if I want to put on a little show for you when you're not home? How am I supposed to do that if I don't know the best position?"

My eyes narrow. "You play dirty. How about I just turn your camera on all the time so you can tease as you wish. I'm sure I'll be happy with any position."

"Wow, I thought that would work."

I zip my lips and then walk to the small table in her room to put her stuff down there. "Now, it's time we have a little talk." I grab her wrist and tug her gently until she presses against me. "My attraction for you isn't new. Since the first time I saw you, I've wanted you. I've been able to get to know you better over the past year, but especially since you've been here. I know your feelings for Aren, and I'm not going to stand in the way of that. If-"

"He doesn't want-"

"If he doesn't want you *with* me, I'll step back. But this is a one time offer. Because once I have my cock in you a second time,

I'm claiming you. I'll share you with him, but if you let me have you again, you need to understand that you're mine and I won't be stepping away from you. I don't know exactly how your conversation went, I understand you think he doesn't want you, but I told you to give him time to come to terms. He has feelings for you, and we forced him to confront them last night. He needs time to sort through all of that on his own. Even though he hurt you today and stepped away, he'll be back. So if you want to wait for him and kick me to the curb, now is your chance. Otherwise, when he comes back for you, you better understand that you're getting both of us then, whether he wants that or not."

"Enzo, he isn't going to come back for me. But even if he does, I want you. I do want both of you, but I want you. I don't want you to think I'm just using you to fill the time or something."

"I don't think that. And I want you. I enjoy sharing and watching, but I don't have to have that. You are what's important." I trace her cheeks.

"How did this happen?" She asks quietly.

"You killed a man and ripped out my fucking heart when you did."

"That's what did it?"

"That was fucking hot as hell. But I think you strutting around my house in those heels really did me in. I have a Pavlovian response to the sound of those heels. Just hearing you coming down the hall makes me hard as a rock."

"That sounds awfully awkward for you."

"It has been. Maybe you should strip down just to those heels and fulfill a little fantasy I've been playing with."

"Wow, diving right into fantasy fulfillment?" Her hands slide down my chest and her cheeks heat. "You know, last night was the first time in a long time. Do you think we could sit all your kink aside for tonight? I'm feeling..." She rolls her shoulders, "exposed?"

Shit. I'm the fucking worst. I thought I was being gentle with her, well, as gentle as I could be when edging her and Aren. I step back from her, putting some space between us while I gather my thoughts. We went from nothing to sexing it up as a show for her step-brother in a matter of days. "Let's eat." I take her hand and drag her from her room.

"What?"

"We are going out. We are getting food. It's a little thing called a date."

"You don't have-"

"Wait!" I stop. "This isn't a kink thing, but you need to put on your heels."

"What?" She shakes her head like I gave her whip-lash.

"Shoes. You need shoes to leave the house, Sunshine."

Lia is wearing her usual confidence as I hold out a hand for her to climb from my car. She's all legs as she takes my hand and stands. With her heels, she's eye level with me, and all her soft places line right up to all of my hard ones. She flashes a wink like she knows exactly what I'm thinking. "Don't get us blown up tonight, okay?" Lia presses a quick kiss to my lips before sneaking the car keys from my other hand and throwing them into the hands of the valet. She grins at the man like she's asking him to bed and I'm surprised he doesn't fall to his knees right there on the street. His eyes flash to mine and then dart away as he walks around my car to move it.

"No promises. Especially if you go around making all the men in our vicinity beg."

"I thought you wanted to watch?"

"I thought this was date night? No kink on date night."

"Oh, setting rules, are we?" She releases my hand when I hold the door to the restaurant open, and I watch the sway of her hips as she walks away from me. When we are seated without giving a name, Lia turns to eye me wearily. "Is this another family business?"

"We have many."

"But we aren't going to get blown up?"

"We can only hope."

"Champagne, I would like champagne please." A wish I can

fulfill with ease. I place an order for a bottle when a server comes to our table to hand us menus.

"So, I know Aren kept the men away, but... how long has it been?"

She leans forward and lowers her voice. "Not to sound like a slut or anything, but one night."

"Adorable. How long, Lia?"

She squirms. "Can we just say years?"

"The more you avoid answering, the more I need to know."

"Fine. I lost my virginity to my high school boyfriend. We did it a few times, and then I moved because my mom got remarried. I was sixteen."

"What the fuck?"

"Yep, perfect reaction." I think of the night before. I prepped her before fucking her. I know I didn't hurt her, but the idea of her basically being a born-again virgin and me taking her like I did last night doesn't sit right with me. No wonder she feels exposed. I seriously messed up. "I don't regret last night." She states like she knows what I'm thinking.

"I don't either. But I could have done better."

"I'm not sure I could have finished any more than I did. You did just fine."

"I knew I liked you for a reason." We order food and the rest of the night plays out like a regular date. Or at least, what I presume a regular date would be. I've never had a normal life, which carried over to any relationships I've had. It doesn't get past me how easy it feels between us. We joke and talk like we've been doing this for years and still enjoy each other's company. Mostly, we avoid discussions of Aren, but Lia brings him up towards the end of dinner as we share a large slice of chocolate cake. She gets chocolate icing on her upper lip and I reach across the table to wipe it free. She watches with widened eyes as I suck the icing off my finger.

"That shouldn't be hot." She whispers with a dangerous smile.

"The hotness comes naturally."

"Does that go hand in hand with the small ego?"

"Nothing about me is small." I quip with ease, enjoying the banter and how she holds her own against me so easily.

"Do you really think Aren wants me? Like, he wasn't just caught up in the moment?" She shifts in her seat and chews on her bottom lip. I don't enjoy seeing her lack her usual confidence, but I understand she needs time.

"I don't think, I know. I read people pretty well, it goes along with the territory. Just give him some time, and until he comes around, you have me to play with."

She gives me a dull stare that makes me chuckle. I wave the server over so that I can pay our bill. Lia tucks her arm in the crook of mine and rests her head on my shoulder as we walk back to the valet for the car. "Thank you, this was really nice."

"You deserve to be wined and dined. I'm glad that you allowed me to do it."

"I thought you just wanted me to be your new hit woman."

"Well, that too. I have all kinds of fun ideas waiting for you." I slide my hand down her back until I reach her firm ass and give it a squeeze. She squeaks in response and it's so unlike her I laugh, ignoring the glare she gives me. I open the car door for her and stand in front of the doorway to block anyone from seeing her in case her short dress plays peekaboo while she slides in. She sings in the car and her voice washes over me. It's the first time I've heard her sing, and it's a travesty that she doesn't walk around the house singing all the time.

"What?" She asks when she catches me glancing her way.

"Your voice is beautiful. I'm offended I haven't heard you singing in the shower or something since you've been staying with me. You blast your music enough."

"What, do you have a camera in the bathroom too? That's sick, Enzo."

"No, I don't have a fucking camera in the bathroom."

"Good, you had me worried a bit there." She blows me a kiss when I glare at her again.

15

Lia

When we get back, Enzo checks in with the guards before sweeping my legs out from under me, gathering me in his arms, laughing when I yelp in surprise. "What are you doing?"

"Carrying my woman to my bedroom. What does it look like I'm doing?" My woman. His claim on me settles a warmth in my chest, which spreads as he holds me tight and carries me to his room like I weigh nothing. His lips crash against mine before we even make it to his room. He tastes like chocolate and wine as his tongue sweeps across mine, stealing my breath. He sits me on the edge of the bed and drops to his knees in front of me, putting my shoe against his chest. I watch in awe as he kisses my knee and then slowly undoes the clasp of my heel and slides it off my foot. He tosses it over his shoulder so nonchalantly that I giggle. Enzo gives my other leg the same care before chucking my other shoe behind him. He doesn't get off his knees, though. Instead, he spreads kisses slowly up my thighs, taking turns with each leg as his fingers inch up until they slip under my dress.

"Lay back, Sunshine. Let me take care of you." Enzo's voice is gravely and desperate. I lay back without a second thought. I feel safe with him, even without Aren in the room with us. His hands continue to slide up the outside of my legs and over my hips before he pulls back to look at me. "It seems you missed something when you got dressed for dinner."

"Did I?" I ask coyly. His hands are big and when he lays them flat on the top of my legs, his thumbs trace to the inside of my thighs, gently caressing my pussy. I'm already wet for him, and he sucks in a breath when he finds that out for himself.

"How long has my woman been needy for me? I would have taken care of you in the middle of the restaurant had I known."

"How would you have done that?" He slides my dress up over my hips and looks at me like he didn't just eat a full meal. Enzo spreads my legs and rubs a finger over my slit. I can hear how wet I am as he moves his finger teasingly, not touching where I need to be touched.

"I would have ordered everyone out of my fucking building and laid you out on the table. That chocolate cake is nothing. I would have devoured you for dinner instead."

"Show me." I gasp as he finally rubs a wet finger over my clit. And he does. His mouth is on me, eating me out like I give him air. I gasp as my whole body goes tense against his mouth, every nerve ending on fire. "Enzo," I grasp his hair and hold his face against me, not even shy in the way I beg for more. His tongue, teeth, and lips dance together until I'm rising off the bed with a cry. Just as I'm tipping over, he fills me with two fingers, curling them deep inside and giving me something to pulse against as I orgasm. "Oh god, Enzo." He slowly moves his fingers in and out, drawing it out for me as he places soft kisses against my skin.

"What a good girl." He pulls me back up so that I'm sitting and reaches behind me to pull the zipper down at my back. He's careful to keep the zipper from getting caught in my hair as he pulls the dress over my head and takes in my naked form. "Fuck, you are stunning." He takes time rubbing his fingers over each of my nipples until they are hard peaks and then leans forward to suck one into his mouth. His tongue twirls over my already sensitive nipple and I cling to him, pressing my own kisses down his neck.

"You make me feel so good. I want you inside me. I'm on birth control... are you..." I don't know the right way to ask this, but I want him without a condom. I want to feel him inside me and have him fill me. He understands well enough though.

"I'm clean. I get tested regularly and I never fuck without a condom. Are you sure you want that? Want me that way?" He actually looks unsure of himself as he asks.

"Yes, please. If you're okay with that? I want you to make a mess of me."

Enzo growls at my words and stands away from me so he can strip. I sit up on my elbows to watch as he undoes each button, exposing more and more tattooed skin as he goes. He's near feral by the time he's undoing his belt. "This is a first for me, Sunshine. I can't wait to feel you while I'm bare inside you. I'm going to watch my come spill out of you and lick you clean after."

"Oh god." I feel like static electricity is running through my veins. My heart races, and my pussy is needy for him all over again. It doesn't matter that he made me come just moments ago.

"You like that, don't you?"

"Yes." It comes out breathy as he climbs over me, all his glorious naked skin touching mine. He holds my legs wide as he fits between them, resting my knees against his sides as he grabs my hips and pulls me forward, lifting me partially off the bed so that I rest on his legs at an angle instead.

"You drive me fucking insane, woman." Enzo takes his heavy cock in hand and rubs his tip against me. I whimper at the feeling, sensitive from what he's already done to me while also half insane with the need to have him inside me. He keeps teasing me though, soaking in the feeling of rubbing against me bare.

"I'll probably feel even better when you're inside me," I half tease, half beg.

Enzo slowly slides in just the tip, continuing to tease me as he draws back out and then slides only slightly deeper, doing it over and over until I groan his name. I'm shaking all over with the need for him to fill me, to fulfill his promise. I've gone years without sex, and until last night, I never orgasmed during sex, but now that I know what I was missing, I feel hungry for more. Finally, he gives in and sinks all the way inside me, moaning my name like a prayer. "Fuck, fuck, fuck.... Lia..." His hands tighten on my hips as he draws back out and then slams into me. "Tell me if I'm too much, but I need to fuck you. You feel too damn good."

"Yes! Please, Enzo." My nails dig into his forearms, holding on for dear life as he gives himself over to his need. Watching him come apart like this drives me wild and I buck against him, needing more and needing him harder. We rush to the finish, any slow teasing long forgotten as we both take and take from one another. I clamp around him but his fingers dig even tighter.

"Hold on for me, Sunshine. I want you to come with me. Hold on." He begs as he holds back his own finish, slamming into me a few more times. "Fuck, now. Come now." And I do. I could barely hold back before, but the moment he gives me permission, I explode around him just as his come fills me. We cry out against each other's skin. Neither of us moves for a while. Both of us catching our breath. Then Enzo lets me go and sits back to watch as he pulls his cock free from me. He still looks half hard and his cock glistens from the both of us. I feel a wetness drip out of me and down my skin and Enzo tracks it with his eyes. He reaches his fingers down and spreads me wide and I feel more of our come seep out of me. Then he moves and puts his face between my legs to finish his promise, licking me clean and groaning with pleasure as he does it. And I'm fucking lost.

16

Aren

Hearing them fuck the night before was bad enough. Enzo, the asshole, left his bedroom door wide open so I could hear clear as day as he took Lia. It took everything in me to keep my dick in my pants and to stay on my side of the door in my room. I wanted to burst down the hallway. I wanted to join them, or grab Lia and drag her to my room instead so I could hear her scream my name. I'm so tired of hearing Enzo's name on her lips, and I'm so tired of knowing he's giving her something that I can't. Fuck. I got no sleep and couldn't even relieve myself in the shower because I knew the second my hand was on my dick my thoughts would go to her, and I was not going to fucking come to my step-sister again. Especially after she told me she wanted me and I told her no.

But watching her and Enzo walk into the kitchen together, freshly fucked and showered, is a whole other torture I wasn't ready for. She's glowing and her smile only barely falters when she spots me. "Morning," Enzo greets me cheerily and I just grunt in response. I want to rip his head off, but I remind myself that Lia said she wanted me, that she wanted us both, and I told her I couldn't do that. She accused me before of making her unhappy, not letting her live her life, and murdering her new boy toy in cold blood certainly wouldn't help those feelings towards me. There was a spread of food already at the table when I gave up on sleep and came into the dining area. From the look in Enzo's fridge, his cook came and prepped some meals already and prepared breakfast for everyone. Lia fills a bowl with fruit and yogurt but steals two slices of bacon and moans around it when she takes her first crispy bite. Enzo and I both go on alert and look at her, watching as she chews and swallows with her eyes closed before blinking them open to find us both staring at her.

"Which do you prefer, Sunshine? The bacon or the chocolate cake?" Enzo asks with a grin. I feel like he's alluding to something that I don't know.

"That's a tough one. Maybe I'd prefer them together." She walks around me without acknowledgement and kisses Enzo. My knuckles go white as I make a fist, but I force myself to release it finger by finger and reach out for my coffee. I already ate while I waited for them to come out of their little love nest.

"Any luck at the club yesterday?" I interrupt them after my sip of coffee.

"I need to check in with Zane. We had a few leads, but I left before we got a definitive answer on anything." His eyes slide to Lia and she avoids looking at me. Did she call him and ask him to come home after we talked? I heard him get back soon after, and then they left together. I don't ask though, I just nod and force myself to sit through this torture. I made my choice, and now I have to live with it. It's not fair of me to put that on Lia. His phone chooses that moment to ring, and he fully releases Lia so he can grab it from the counter. I watch her as she starts to eat and wonder how the hell she killed someone. I can't imagine it. She's always been tough, but the idea of her slamming her dagger into someone, of her being covered in blood, blows my mind. And it's not lost on me that it's my fault she was in that position. If I hadn't been so hard on her since our parents died, so protective of her, she wouldn't have felt the need to sneak out. She probably would have taken a bodyguard if she even felt the need to go out.

And she ended up right in Enzo's arms because of that attack. I eye the two of them as they move around one another with ease while he talks on the phone and I feel sick. Protecting her from all the danger that surrounded us was always my top priority, but as I watch her grin at Enzo and feel the flair of jealousy, I allow myself to be honest. I also wanted to keep her for myself. Her soft gaze flicks to me and I hold it. I need some contact with her before I push these dark thoughts away again. I can't have her. I'll just have to keep reminding myself and try not to kill myself knowing Enzo is winning her. I drag my eyes away from hers and look to Enzo as he puts his phone on the counter.

"He has some footage he's sending over and wants Lia and I to see if we recognize the guy."

"Were any connections made for the guy that attacked Lia?"

I follow them to Enzo's office space. "Not yet. He didn't have ID on him when he went after Lia but they took pics of him for us to match him. Zane's had people looking into it."

"I'll try to kill them a little less next time so you guys can question him."

"There won't be a next time." I growl towards her while Enzo just chuckles.

"Nah, you murder away, we'll figure it out on our end. Can't have you holding back those claws." He reaches out and touches a spot on her wrist, rubbing gently before pulling away. She avoids looking at me as she takes a seat in front of his desk, leaving the chair beside her open for me. His office has more character than I've seen from the rest of his house. Everything is dark, dark green walls, dark wood shelves and desk, but then the back wall is filled with glass looking out into a garden I didn't even know he had. Enzo pulls his chair to the other side of Lia and turns his computer screen and keyboard around so we can all see the screen.

"This is the man that tried to attack Lia." Enzo fills the screen with the slack face of a dead man. Flecks of blood are splattered on his skin. His eyes are a dull blue, staring blankly ahead, his jaw has a spattering of hair that matches the brown on his head. There's nothing significant about him. He's on the young side but that doesn't mean anything. He might be more impressionable, able to get pulled into the wrong side of things with the promise of some extra money and prestige. "It's already been sent to the contacts on your side so they can look into him too." He reads my mind and I just give a grunt in response. Then I look over at my step-sister. I've done all I can to protect her from the darker part of our world, but she was attacked and she took the life of someone else. Even in self-defense, I know that leaves a mark. She stares into the face of her attacker. He caught her unawares and alone. He could have ripped her from this world, from me, if she hadn't jumped to her own defense.

I reach over and take her hand when I see just how pale she is while staring at the photo. "How about the video footage?" I ask, hoping Enzo picks up on my silent signal to move along. He glances at me and then Lia and quickly looks away to type. He fills the screen with grainy footage. The camera is facing the club, but it's across the street. I can see the doors; the bouncer stands in front of him, a burly man that can barely bring his hands together in front of him. I can't really make out his features, just the size of him. A man comes on the screen, walking slowly down the sidewalk looking at the club. A couple has their IDs checked and then the bouncer opens the doors for them. The man on the sidewalk pulls something from his sweatshirt and throws it between the bouncer's legs. It rolls into the building and the man takes off running. The bouncer doesn't even have time to react before the explosion happens. My jaw aches from how hard I grind my teeth together. Lia had been inside that building. I have no idea how close she was to where the explosion took place, but I squeeze her hand, needing to feel that she's still here.

"He was in a hoodie, are there any other angles? Other cameras from where he came from?"

"Sure thing. We have a few here." Enzo clicks the next one, and this one shows his face. It's before he pulls up his hood and turns the corner of the block. Enzo freezes the picture at the best angle and saves it as an image before moving to the final video. This shows him running away before jumping in a car before it speeds away. We pause for plates but there aren't any. Enzo goes back to save a shot of the car and the shadow of the driver. He fills the screen with the three images, the first attacker, and then our second guy and the get-away car.

"He's young too." Lia says, squinting at the man. "He has a tattoo on his neck," she points at the screen, and I take a harder look at the ink peeking out from where he's pulling the hood up.

"Good eye, Sunshine." Enzo pulls that video again and goes through it frame by frame to see if he can get a clearer shot of the ink. There's only one spot that gives a better image.

"A bird maybe? It looks like a wing coming from the front." Lia leans back while Enzo saves that image too.

"Well, he never stepped foot in the club, so we didn't even bump arms with him while we were there. I don't know him. You guys?"

I look at the man carefully, the dark eyes and hair, the lines of the tattoo. This man walked. He put Lia in danger and then walked away. I don't recognize him, but I file away every detail of him. I want to know that I could simply glance at him in a sea of people and recognize him.

"Oh..." Lia lets go of my hand and leans forward. She stares hard at the screen until I worry she'll go cross-eyed. Then she slams her eyes shut and holds up a hand before either of us can ask her what she's doing. "Has Mara seen these?"

"I'm sure Zane has shown her, but I don't know for sure." Enzo waits for her to give more info, but I look back at the photo and try to see what she's seeing.

"We went to a lot of events with Hayk towards the end. He liked to put on an appearance and talk shit. Even better if he could make Mara go to show her off and put his gross hands on her. He had his few guards that followed him around, but he had a few others too that we'd see around sometimes. They were all on the younger side, stupid. Some of them were even stupid enough to sneak past Aren and hit on me."

"Excuse me?" I thunder.

She just waves me away. "I'm not certain, but maybe Mara

would be. But I think he was one of Hayk's, I'm pretty sure he got a little handsy with my ass at one of the dinners they never fed us at."

"Once again, excuse me? What the fuck, Lia? Why didn't you say something?"

She just shrugs. "I told him to back off, and he did. Didn't really seem worth it."

"Fuck that. I get to kill this one. I'm going to shove his dick in his mouth while he's still alive."

"Remind me not to piss you off." Enzo mumbles.

I just stare at him. "Too late for that, asshole." He returns my silent threat with a grin.

"Okay, I'm sending this to Mara to look at. Maybe she'll have a name. But if we think he's connected to Hayk, we at least have a direction to head in. Nice work."

17

Enzo

Two days later, we have a name. I wake tangled around Lia, our legs wrapped around each other, a blanket twisted between us. Her breasts are bare and pressed against my chest and her breath comes out in gentle little puffs. My phone pings and I know I need to get it and see what's up. Before we tumbled into bed last night, Zane told me he was sending an enforcer after one Chris Balian. I'm sure the message says that he's been found and Zane wants to know if I want in on the questioning. But Lia's soft body is on mine, and the thought of violence is so far from my mind right now. She hasn't gone back to her bed but shares mine each night. I'm not one that often has repeats, but things are very different with her. I pull her closer where I would already be kicking others out the door. Aren is chipping away each day. I'm not sure that she sees it, but his gaze follows her every move, and he watches me take her to my room each night. He just stands there until we cross my threshold. Last night, he took a step towards us before turning and slamming his door. The man is an idiot.

Lia lets out a little whimper in her sleep, and I stiffen at the sound. Even in sleep, it sounds so sad that I want to rip someone's head off. "Shh, Sunshine. I've got you." I brush a thumb across her cheekbone and wonder how these women pull us under their spells. Mara had Zane wrapped around her little finger after he saw her once, maybe twice. I may have known Lia longer, but she stopped my heart the moment I saw her standing over that body, looking put out by his interruption.

I decide to ignore my phone for a bit longer and pull the blanket from our bodies. I spread her legs and wake her with some gentle kisses. On her pussy. I can tell when she wakes up. She stiffens for just a moment before completely relaxing again and letting out a moan as I spear her with my tongue. I haven't closed my bedroom door once since she's been with me. I know she wants Aren too. He has to come to her on his own this time, but I'm at least leaving the invitation open for him. Lia doesn't hold back on her volume, in fact, I'm pretty sure she's always sure to be extra loud every time I give her an orgasm. I love her for it.

Shit. Can't think of a word like that. Especially while my tongue is buried in her and she's riding my face. I grip her hips hard and jerk her forward so she can rub against me harder. "Enzo! I'm so close. Please," she pants and reaches her arms behind her to press her hands against the headboard. I replace my tongue with fingers and I suck her clit hard and feel as she comes around my fingers. I let her ride it out before I lick her clean and then I sit up.

"Open your mouth, Sunshine." She does as I command and I smile my approval before giving her my fingers to suck clean. She swirls her tongue around them before sucking hard and I imagine her doing the same move to my cock, but I need to check my phone now. As much as it pains me to give Zane any attention while I'm rocking a hard on. "You can go back to sleep now. I have work to do." I grin at her as she shoots me a glare, but she doesn't argue when I pick up my phone to look at my messages. She knows we had the name last night, so she knows what's coming, well, besides her.

"They've got him. Why don't you sway that naked ass to get Aren out of bed? He already called dibs on this guy." She's still glaring at me but I give her a dare. "Go on, baby. I'm sure he's already awake. You scream my name across my house so beautifully."

"You're such an ass sometimes."

"Shit, need to bring up my game if it's only sometimes." I slap her ass when she stands, but she is the perfect temptress. She throws on my shirt, which barely covers her ass, and marches out of my room to summon Aren. Fuck, if that woman isn't the most fun I've ever had.

I hear her knock on his door so I move to stand in the doorway to watch. I'm naked but the angle of my door covers me at least, not that he hasn't watched me go balls deep in Lia, anyway. For all I know, he's been sneaking to stand outside my door while I fuck her each night. He opens the door and I curse not being able to see his face because he doesn't step out far enough. She sways back towards me and his door slams shut.

"He'll be ready in ten." She has a little sparkle in her eye and I know his face must have been perfect.

Lia insists on coming along but says she'll stay out of the room. She doesn't want to be left alone and hopes Mara will end up being there. Aren is wound so tight I'm tempted to find a stick to poke him with just to see if he'll burst. I almost feel bad for the man locked away, because Aren's got a lot of pent up energy he's ready to expel. He's practically breathing violence as I drive. It's kind of fucking distracting, actually. I pull up to the warehouse we use for these kinds of parties, give a quick wave to the guards, and park. Aren hardly waits for the car to turn off before he's out of it and marching towards the building.

Lia worries her lip as she watches him but I just shrug. "He knows you'd miss my dick if he cut it off, but he's got free rein on this guy. Are you sure you want to be here for this?" I know he's kept her away from the darkest bits of our lives, but if Zane gives him the okay, Aren is going to go feral on this dude.

"If the guy was willing to blow me up, I'm willing to watch Aren beat him to death."

"Fair enough, Sunshine." I take her hand and lead her

towards the warehouse. One of the muscles we trust pulls the door aside for Aren so we follow him in before I take the lead. The front of the warehouse is a bit of a maze of doors to ensure we have time to escape in case of a breech. After two doors, Aren stops and pulls Lia away from me. I almost protest, until he glares my way in silent warning; so I take a few steps to give them time alone. I'm sure he wants to beg her to stay away, but maybe he doesn't know our girl as well as he thinks he does. They share a few harsh whispers before she yanks her arm away and turns a sugary sweet smile on me. The woman saunters to my side and loops her arm in mine.

I lean down so I can brush against her ear and whisper, "I feel so used right now." She just tilts her head up to me to show me her full smile. "Don't lie; I know you like it." Then she kisses my cheek while I'm still leaning towards her. I reach down to grab her ass and chuckle at her squeal of surprise. After a few more doors, I find Zane and Mara sitting at a small table sipping coffees, looking the same as they might while sitting at their own kitchen counter. Mara's eyes instantly go to where my arm is wrapped around her cousin and her gaze narrows. Worry slams into me. Shit. Should I have told Lia about my night with Mara? It had all been in good fun, just a one time thing over a year ago. Mara's husband had been an active participant, so it's not like anything shady happened. But. I slept with her, and now I'm sleeping with Lia. Cold washes through my veins at the thought of Lia thinking less of me because of what we did. She knows I like to share sometimes and that I like to watch, but she probably wasn't expecting me to have slept with her cousin.

"Where is he?" Aren's demand breaks my dark cycle and I give Lia's hip a small squeeze before I release her. Lia glides over to pull Mara into a tight hug before taking up the seat beside her.

"Right through there," Zane nods towards the door on the other side of the room. It's thick metal, blocking out any sounds our guest might be making.

"Let's go." Aren stalks towards the door, but Zane just lifts two fingers, which brings Aren to a stop. No matter our relation and friendships, Zane and Mara are now head of both our houses. They are the most powerful players on the board, and all of us know to follow any orders they give, even silent ones.

"He is one of Hayk's." Mara speaks up now, eyeing the door with trepidation. "We thought we cleaned house well enough when we took over, but a few of his men disappeared after Hayk went missing and my father claimed he'd taken him out. By the time Zane and I took over, there were ones we couldn't find a trace of."

"So now they've come out to play." I say, crossing my arms as I try to work out how many would have gotten away before we started our purge. There was a nice gap of time between Mara killing Hayk and taking out her father. We'd been focused on the moves we needed to make to bring her father out, I don't think any of us were too worried over some random men Hayk once ruled over.

"We want to find out how many more made a run for it. Is someone ruling over them, ordering them to come after us, or are there just a few stragglers trying to play a game they don't have big enough balls for?"

"Excuse you," Mara glares at her husband. "I do just fine without any balls. Also, vaginas can take a beating and bring life into this world, while tapping balls a little too hard brings men to their knees, so tell me again who really has the power?"

"I don't know, baby. Maybe I'll try out that beating theory later and see how much you can take-"

"Okay, ew. There are other people present in this room Zane. Mafia boss or not, I'll need you to keep it in your pants for a hot minute until the rest of us leave the room."

Aren mumbles something that I don't quite catch, but I can tell by the look on his face he's very much over all of us. "Great, anything else we need to beat out of the punk before I rip him to shreds?"

"Aren, what's wrong?" Mara frowns at her cousin. Instead of answering, he pushes the door open and steps into the darkness beyond. Mara's gaze flicks to Lia, who gives a little shrug. "I thought I recognized the guy as one of Hayk's men that used to hit on me sometimes at parties. I let that slip and now Aren's all protective and pissed."

"That's the least of his current issues." I add. "You ladies good sitting out here?"

"What," Mara bats her eyelashes at me. "I don't get to play? I like a bit of dismemberment as much as the next lady."

"I think Aren's claimed all dismemberment on this one." Lia giggles and leans back in her chair. "I'm good. Blood is gross. I don't want to lose another pair of shoes."

18

AREN

I let Zane take the lead on asking the questions, but I don't let either of the other men lay a hand on the kid. He's all mine. I relish the feel of my knuckles swelling from hitting him over and over, the splatter of blood that dots my skin, and the pull of muscles from using my body to harm another gives me solace. It's not often I get my hands dirty, but I need this. It's a bit dangerous how often I imagine Enzo's face instead of the one in front of me as I pound my fists into him. But this man tried to lay a hand on Lia without her consent. He flirted with her, put his eyes on her, and tried to take something that didn't belong to him. Then he almost killed her with his little stunt at the club. I don't care about anything else. I don't care if he has a whole gang of men hidden away to do his bidding. I only care about Lia. She could have been hurt. She could have died.

I don't even listen to the answers he gives or the questions Zane and Enzo throw at him. I just wait for the small nod Zane gives to tell me it's time to throw another punch. Or break another bone. I'm like one of the hired men whose only purpose is to cause pain to our enemies. For the first time, I understand the appeal. It's very cathartic. I remember how Lia looked outside my room this morning in Enzo's shirt. It wasn't buttoned all the way, and it was all too easy to see the swell of her breasts. Her nipples were sharp points begging for me to touch. Her hair mussed from sleep and the orgasm Enzo had given her. She's mine. Lia should be wearing my shirt. She should be screaming my name.

"Aren." Zane's sharp voice cuts through my thoughts and I realize I just punched my new *friend* Chris right in the stomach before Zane had given a command. I give a quick, sheepish nod and take a step back. Enzo is grinning ear to ear at me. He knows too much. He knows what he's doing to me. I wonder if I can get away with slipping and punching him square in the face.

Zane gives Chris a minute to catch his breath before he asks again. "Where is Hayk's cousin hiding?"

"I don't fucking know! He sends his orders, we follow them. None of us have seen him since Hayk's death. Vram was quick to take over after Hayk disappeared, but with Erik Papazian claiming Hayk made a move against him, it wasn't safe for Vram to be seen. He was afraid someone would come after him for revenge. Then you and the girl-"

Zane gives his little nod of command, so I step forward and throw a punch right into Chris' face. My knuckles scream from slamming into teeth, but seeing blood gush out of his mouth and watching him spit out two teeth makes it all worth it. "You will speak of my wife, head of the Papazian family, with the respect she deserves. If you don't, I'll let her in here to cut out your tongue. Is that understood?" Zane's tone is a dark promise and the kid nods. "Good, you may continue."

"Vram knew he couldn't come out of hiding when the two of you took over. That didn't stop him from biding his time and was ready to make some moves against you. But I haven't seen him. I have no idea where he is. I'm just one of the runners."

"Sounds like you have nothing else to give us then. And it doesn't sound like you'll be missed." Zane looks at me, giving me all the permission to finish the job.

"No! Please! I told you everything I know!"

"And now you have to deal with the choices you've made." Zane turns his back and leaves the room. Enzo gives me a quick nod and leaves me alone with my punching bag.

The ladies are caught up with the information we got by the time I leave the room, and Zane and Mara look ready to go. Lia looks me over and I notice her lips form a small line, but she doesn't say anything. Enzo has his arm draped over her shoulder and they sit side by side at the table. I feel raw after letting all my aggression out. I feel broken in a way I haven't felt since my father died and I knew I was the only thing standing between Lia and death. Her soft look pushes me over the edge. I just want to sink into her. For once, I want to lay down my sword and find peace.

Everyone leaves the warehouse together. A cleaning crew passes us, on their way to find the mess I've left behind. Instead of walking next to Enzo, Lia walks behind him and I realize she's staying close to me. She's too good for me. She's too good for this world.

"There's a shower and a change of clothes through here." Zane stops and nods towards a door. "Don't want to go walking around in the wild looking like you do. Don't worry, it's clean and stocked well." I look down at myself and nod. Zane gives me the directions through the doors to find my way out once I'm done. Lia looks like she might say something, but whatever it is, I'm not ready to hear it, so I disappear through the door and rush through a shower. There's a locker filled with different sizes of clothing, so I grab some that fit and put my own clothes in one of the bags they have. Zane apparently has a whole murder set up going on.

I leave the room and find Lia leaning against the far wall, put together as always. She doesn't say anything, just pulls away from the wall and starts towards the doorway Zane told me to go through. "Do you need a first-aid kit or anything?" She finally asks after our third door.

I glance down at my knuckles but stretch my fingers out and shake my head. "I'm fine." But I'm not fine. I won't be fine until I have her, the other part of my fucking soul. But I stay silent as Enzo drives us back to his house. By the time he parks, the need inside me is a wildfire burning through any reason I have for not claiming her. Enzo eyes me before turning to Lia. "If you're good, I'm going to run over to Zane's just to go over some next steps. You guys can stay and relax, it's been a long day." Lia nods and kisses him before getting out of the car, but I stay until she's shut the door. Enzo stares at me. "It's about time you've come around. But know this, I'm not letting her go. I have no problems sharing her however she wants to be shared, but I'm not stepping aside. And if you hurt her like you did the last time, I'll make you disappear."

He'd never do that, because it would hurt Lia if anything happened to either of us. But I let him have his upper hand for now and climb out without a word. Lia falls into step beside me but doesn't reach for me or speak. We've always had an ease between us. We move naturally around one another, a dance through this world that only we know. Some of that ease is gone, replaced with tension, but I'm ready to put a stop to that.

"Are you okay?" Lia breaks the silence as we move to the hallway with the bedrooms. I stop outside my door and look at her.

"No. I haven't fucking been okay since I left you, and you had to kill a man to save yourself."

"Aren-"

"Lia. It's been my job to protect you all these years. You might hate it, but you needed me. We were alone, and I had to protect you. Our world is so dangerous, but it was so much worse when our parents died. But if you think I haven't noticed you all these years, you'd be very wrong." I grab her and turn our bodies so she's pressed against my door, my arms on either side of her. Her eyes widen, but she doesn't argue or try to move away from me. "Sure, I kept the men away because none of them were good enough for you, but more because you've always been mine." I tilt her chin up so we are eye-to-eye. "You've always been mine." Any shield I had up against my feelings for her are gone. I beat them out of me as I took a man's life with my bare hands. I look down at her full lips and groan when she sucks in her bottom lip. Leaning down is as easy as breathing, and she leans forward to meet me. It's just a soft brushing of lips. A taste. But she melts against me so easily. She's all soft as she presses against me, she accepts my possession so easily. I pull back from her lips and brush my fingers over her cheekbones, over her lips, down her neck. "I'm so pissed Enzo has been inside you. That he's tasted you as you come. Some really dark part of me wants to slit his throat and take you right there, next to his body." I can hear her swallow as her eyes go wide with fear. I let out a long sigh. "You really like him, don't you?"

"I do." Her voice is soft, but her hard determination is in those two words. She's claiming him as much as I'm claiming her.

"Hmm, guess we'll keep him too. But if he ever does anything to hurt you, he will disappear from this earth." I use his own threat against him.

"We'll... we'll keep him?" She giggles against me, her cheeks going pink.

I put my hands back against the door on either side of her head, surrounding her in a gentle reminder that it's me currently standing with her. "Sure, he can be like... a puppy or something." I tease her.

"Aren," her eyes dart between mine and she wets her lips again. I have a feral need to suck on that tongue. "What are we doing?"

"We are doing what we always do, Lia. We are being a team. You and me. And I guess Enzo."

"So, what, are we dating now?"

"If that's what you want to call it." I nip at the side of her neck before sucking on the soft skin there. Her back arches away from the door and it takes all the power in me to let her speak again.

"And, I'm also dating Enzo?"

"You are mine, but I will never deny you something that brings you happiness. Even if it's more shoes. Even if it's Enzo. I can share with him only because you want him."

"And-" I put a finger over her lips to stop this torture.

"That's enough talking right now. You can't overthink this. I want you. And I want you happy. Apparently, I've done a poor job of that in the past, but I'm able to change. If something makes you unhappy, you come to me and I'll deal with it. Otherwise, you just do what you want, and I'll be at your side."

"One more question?" She asks too sweetly, but I nod anyway to allow it. "Did you enjoy watching me with Enzo?"

Fuck. I try to blink away the memory of how hard I was that night watching them. "Yes. You are incredibly sexy and it was a wonderful show you put on for me. But now, I need a taste of my own." I scoop her up and throw open my door, letting it bang against the wall. I don't bother to close it. I know Enzo will give us some time alone together, and when he gets back, I guess we are going with an open door policy. An open invitation. I toss her on the bed and take in my prize. "You better be on a pill or some shit, because I'm not fucking you with a condom. Nothing is coming between us. Are you good with that?"

"Yes." The single word is more of a squeak and I take some manly pride in that. I'm already so hard for her. I need to be inside her, but I'm also not going to rush this. She's already had her mouth on me, but I haven't had my taste.

19

LIA

He actually rips through my clothes. Not even on the seams, but right through the middle. Then his mouth is on me. He licks between my breasts, his hands spread my legs wide so he can fit between them. Then he sucks on one of my nipples until I arch against him, the shock of it going right between my legs. He doesn't ease me into anything. He just takes and takes, marking me as his with every nip and suck against my skin.

"Right now, you only say my name, you got that?"

"Yes, Aren."

"I've heard you scream another man's name far too much. Now it's my turn. Next time you see him, I want you to stutter over his name with a hoarse voice." He cuts himself off as he moves to suck on the side of my neck. Oh... Oh this is dangerous. If this becomes a competition between Aren and Enzo trying to out-sex each other, I'm a dead woman. But fuck, what a way to go. I know he's leaving hickies all over me and it gives me some kind of giddy joy to know he has some need to mark me. Aren moves down my body and gives me a wicked grin when he licks the inside of my thigh and discovers I'm ticklish there.

"What's wrong, Lia?"

"Nothing-" I try to squirm away from him but he does it again, and I burst out laughing, kicking to move away from him.

"Do. Not. Move." He demands, his eyes pinning me to the bed. I go still at his order and the darkness that's taken over. His hands are still gentle against my skin, but nothing in his tone leaves room for me to argue. Enzo's words about Aren being a daddy dom comes back to me, and I bite my lip as the temptation to call him daddy rises. But then he breathes over my pussy. "Already so wet for me, baby." I whimper as his tongue swipes through my center. His fingers dig into my soft skin, and then he *devours*. Aren groans against my most sensitive places, and my fingers go to his hair. I grab the strands and pull, keeping him against me. I break his order when my thighs close around his ears as the pleasure washes over me. "Say my fucking name, baby." He stares up at me as he plunges his fingers inside me, curling them before leaning forward again to suck on my clit.

The gentle waves of pleasure turn sharp, and I scream his name. I claw at his skin, unsure if I want to push him away or pull him closer. He only goes harder through, his fingers working me until my orgasm is done. "You look so beautiful covered in my marks." His gaze takes in my prone form, and then he reaches out to trace each hickey he left behind.

"I thought only teenagers left hickeys?" I tease him.

"I warned you that if you were mine, really mine, it would have consequences. You'll be covered in my marks from now on. I'll find new and creative ways to claim you." I watch as he reaches to stroke himself. He's so hard it looks like it must be painful for him. But his hands move unhurried over his cock. I remember the taste of him in my mouth, the heavy feel of him against my tongue, and he groans when I lick my lips at the memory. "Do you want me? You want to feel my cock take this pussy?"

There's always been a quiet darkness to Aren. His emotions are usually tucked behind a mask unless he's with our small circle of people. But right now, that darkness has a fire of its own. "Yes, please, Aren. Please." I touch him, and that sends him forward, spreading my legs and setting them at his hips. He takes his time though. My Aren wants to tease. He moves his hardness over me, spreading my wetness and rubbing against my sensitive clit. He repeatedly teases at my entrance but doesn't push in. The sounds I make aren't natural. I'm pulsing with need even though I just came. But I need more. I need him. Then he teases me with just his tip, dipping into my warmth before drawing back out and rubbing against me again. I lose count of the times he does this, but his eyes never leave mine as he tortures me. The control he has irritates me. I want him feral. I want him to need me as much as I need him. I've needed him for years and now he's so close, but won't take what I'm so willing to give.

"Come on, Aren. Show me what I've been missing. Stop being a tease; give me what I want." I throw the words at him like a taunt. He surges forward and grabs my wrists, pinning them to the bed above my head.

"You were being such a good girl for me and you've gone and ruined it, Lia. You don't get to tell me what you want, not tonight. Not after screaming another man's name so loud I could hear it in my room. You've been playing dirty since I got here. You've been the fucking tease. And if you think this has been torture, you've underestimated me. You have no idea how long I can draw this out. I've been waiting years to take you. And I've been hearing you get fucked by another man. I'll take my damn time, and you'll fucking be grateful for whatever I choose to give you. Understood?"

Daddy Dom. I give my last itch to be rebellious room to breathe, and smile at him with all the sweetness of a candy shop. "Okay, Daddy. I'll be your good little toy."

"Fucking right, you will be." And he slams into me. The sudden fullness makes me cry out and I'm not sure if it's with joy of finally having him inside me, or just from being overwhelmed by the sensation. He tilts his hips to slam into me again, but then he releases my wrists and straightens once more, watching the sight of his cock getting lost inside me. And then he fucking draws out and goes back to rubbing against me. Oh fuck.

His edging continues for so long I have no sense of time. He takes turns slamming into me, riding me right to the brink, and then pulls out. Over and over. I'm coated with sweat. Every nerve in my body is on fire with the need to come, or pass out, or just fucking die. Anything to end this. "My poor darling. Are those tears for me, baby?" I don't even realize I'm crying until he reaches forward and wipes a drop away. I feel so raw and exposed, even more than I did that first night with the two of them. I'm shaking and I can't stop.

"Please, Aren." The two words come out choked, and he brushes fingers over my sensitive lips.

"Do you need to come, Lia? Do you need me to let you get there?" I nod. It's all I have the energy for. My body is no longer mine. It's all his, for him to use as he pleases. Only he gets to decide if I get to come or not again tonight. Enzo is always trying to see how many times he can get me to finish before I can't take any more. Aren has chosen a unique form of torture. I never truly understood edging until tonight. Aren doesn't make me beg anymore, though. He finally takes me and doesn't stop. He folds my legs up so the back of my knees rest on the insides of his elbows, and he holds me right where he wants as he takes me so deeply that I'm sure I'll feel him for days. I've felt an orgasm rise so many times tonight that I almost fear it this time. Will he actually let me come, or will he pull away again? I think something within my soul will break if he pulls away again.

"Aren, oh Aren. Please-" He releases one of my legs and his finger barely brushes against my clit before I come so hard I actually think I black out. I feel it in every part of my body and I burst into tears from relief. Aren pulls out and comes all over the top of my pussy, drenching me in him. I'm a shaking, sweaty mess. I'm drenched from a mixture of his and my own come, and I can feel the tears streaming non-stop down my cheeks.

"Shh, I've got you." Aren lays down beside me and gathers me into his arms. I cry and shake against his chest while he holds me, tracing gentle fingers down my spine and whispering calming promises against my hair. "That's it, baby." He reassures me when the tears finally stop. I can't even explain this reaction I'm having, but I feel so strung out I'm not sure I have anything left in me. Then he's moving the both of us, keeping me gathered in his arms as he walks us to his bathroom and sits at the edge of the tub with me in his lap. Aren fills the bath with steaming water and drops something inside of it that gives a burst of scented lavender. I arch away from the hot water at first, but he climbs in behind me and keeps me wrapped against him. I end up melting back against his chest and let his fingers trace gentle lines and circles over my skin as I adjust to the warmth of the water.

"You never need to worry, Lia. I'll always take care of you. I'll always make sure you are cared for and looked after." His soft kiss against the side of my neck nearly breaks me again. Then he gets to work with a washcloth. He covers it in some body wash that smells the same as the bubbles in the bath. I let him wash every inch of me. I'm actually not very helpful at all, barely able to lean forward so he can get my back and rinse my hair. Finally, when I feel like I'm going to drift off to sleep sitting up, Aren stands. Water pours off of his naked form, but I can't even find it in me to appreciate the sight of him. He stands me up and dries me carefully with a plush towel and then slips a long shirt over my head before shuffling us both to his bed. But then he pauses.

"Sleep." I say the one word as a plea and he turns to grin at me a bit sheepishly.

"We... made a bit of a mess of my bed. I don't know where clean sheets are. We can sleep in your room." He lifts me again and I don't protest. I just curl up, resting my head in the crook of his neck. I feel the soft mattress and the cool sheets. Then the warmth of his body pressing against me from behind. "Is Enzo home?" I wonder as I drift off.

20

Enzo

Lia wakes slowly. I watch as her breathing changes and her eyelashes flutter. She snuggles in closer to Aren and her fingers twitch within my hold. Aren has his arm draped over her stomach, and he pulls her back against him even though he already warned me she needs some recovery time after the night they had. She gives a soft, tempting moan as Aren brushes his lips over the exposed part of her shoulder. She blinks her eyes open and freezes when she sees me. This will be the real test now that she has Aren.

Relief hits me like a bullet when she gives me a loopy grin. "Enzo," she pulls me closer so that she's happily cocooned between us both. "I missed you." She kisses my jaw and then turns her head to Aren and kisses his lips. Then she settles back against her pillow with a happy little grin still on her lips. Pure sunshine. "You weren't here when I fell asleep." She says to me, though her eyes are closed again.

"No, sorry about that. But Aren invited me to sleep here with the two of you when he saw me get home."

This makes her smile even bigger. "You did?" She asks Aren.

"You asked for him before you fell asleep." He grumbles.

"You big softy." She turns to kiss him again and then gives me a conspiratorial look. "He's kind of mean in bed though."

My muscles tense and my eyes dart over her head to look at him. But he's got his eyes closed in ease. "Excuse me?" I demand.

Lia lets out a long yawn. "He wouldn't let me come. I'm not sure, but I think it was hours, Enzo."

She misses my sigh of relief that she hadn't meant something else. "Oh no, you poor thing. Did he edge you?"

Lia pouts at me and nods, but the flush of her cheeks tells me when he finally did let her go, it had been worth it. He clearly took care of her afterwards, too. Aren's arm pulls her closer again, and he gives her ear an affectionate nip. "You were being bratty and demanding. I hope you learned your lesson."

"She's not bratty with me." I tease.

"That's because you spoil her. Sometimes it's good to wait for the pleasure. To draw it out."

"Hmm... I usually just give her another one to remind her how good it feels. But if you can only give one orgasm, then I guess you have to make it last."

Lia's small burst of laughter earns her what I suspect is a pinch to her butt cheek with the way she squeals and tries to pull away from Aren. Oh yeah, this is going to be so much fun. "Well, since it sounds like the two of you had an active night, I'll go down and grab breakfast and bring it up here. We can all have breakfast in bed before we deal with the real world."

"Did Zane have anything to say about plans?" Aren asks, lifting his head. Zane and I spoke business last night, but we mostly shot the shit while I gave Lia time alone with Aren. I knew they needed it. I could see that some wall came crumbling down in Aren while he beat that rat into a pulp.

"A bit. Knowing who is behind all these attacks makes it easier for us to plan our moves, but he wanted to wait for everyone to be together before we made any final decisions." I head downstairs knowing it won't take long for me to gather supplies for breakfast in bed. My cook always comes early in the morning to prepare breakfast and then fill my fridge with some fresh food for the rest of the day. I like to eat out while I'm checking on how things are running so I don't need much after breakfast usually. Sure enough, I find a beautiful spread of eggs, bacon, and hash-browns set on warming trays as well as fresh fruit and miniature cranberry muffins. I fix up three plates and set them on a tray. Then I pour coffees for each of us and prepare them to everyone's liking. Aren drinks his black like a regular psycho, while Lia likes hers iced with hazelnut creamer. Mine is the traditional cream and sugar. Easy enough.

When I enter the room with the large tray in my hands I find the two of them still in the bed but sitting up. I pause at the ease between them as Aren runs a brush through Lia's long blond hair. Her head is tilted back, her eyes closed in simple ecstasy. Aren sees me first and flashes a smug grin. "Look, she can be a good girl for me too when she wants to be." Her eyes snap open at that, and she turns on him, throwing a punch into his shoulder. "Never mind; I take it back. Always a brat."

"I am picking up on some brat vibes." I tease as I pull the legs for the tray out and sit it at the center of the bed.

"You know, before you take his side, you should ask how our conversation went last night." Lia blinks at me and I freeze. I told her and Aren that I was not going to walk away, not now. Aren inviting me to sleep with them and the ease between all of us this morning made me feel like this was happening as a happy little thrupple, but if she doesn't want me anymore? Can I just walk away? Or will I rage and demand blood? "Aren said we could keep you-"

"Lia," Aren tries to interrupt.

"Like a puppy. He wants to keep you as our little pet." She raises her eyebrows at me and waits for my reaction.

I give my heart a minute to slow before I turn a grin on Aren. "Wow man, kinky. Let me ask, what kind of collar should I buy? I feel like you are a stud guy, black leather. Who will walk me? Is that something you want to do, or do you want to watch Lia-"

"Just... just stop." Aren shakes his head before reaching for his coffee. Lia goes for the fruit, still bouncy from the chaos she's causing.

"I mean, I'm willing to discuss any and all desires." I pluck a piece of bacon from one of the plates. "I'm very committed to this relationship, and I don't want anyone to be shy talking about what they want."

Aren gives me a hard stare as Lia's cheeks turn pink. "Unless Lia is interested in walking you around on a leash, I think I'll pass. I think she's probably sore. I wouldn't mind watching you kiss her better."

"I'd love to, Daddy."

Lia's flaming cheeks crack into a huge grin as she throws her head back and laughs. "Wait," Aren holds up a hand, "what is the deal with this daddy thing you two are doing?"

"Lia, please tell me you called him daddy last night."

"I-" she shakes her head and covers her mouth to stem her laughter. "Maybe."

"Oh, fuck yes." I grab her ankle and twist her so her legs hang over the bed on my side. She has on Aren's shirt, but nothing else, and her beautiful long legs make a tempting sight, leading my eyes right to her center. "You *are* a good girl. And good girls get to *be* breakfast. "

"Seriously, what is the daddy thing between you two?" Aren demands again, seemingly unfazed by my manhandling of our woman.

"It's not us, it's you." I shrug my shoulders and then kneel next to the bed. I go slowly, working my hands up the inside of her legs and spread them for me. I take in the multiple hickies on her body and shake my head at Aren's little claim over her. That's fine, he can leave his marks, but I know I don't need them to make my own claim. Lia's eyes are on mine and I hold her gaze as my thumbs rub gently at the top of her thighs. "Was he cruel to you last night? Did he make you beg?"

She chews on her lip and gives a small nod. I tut at him but Aren just rolls his eyes. "Yeah, but I made her come before we started, and I guarantee she blacked out when I finally let her come at the end." He takes a bite of his eggs like none of this is phasing him.

Her center is puffy and pink and I think she could probably

use a cool bath to soak in. My fingers are gentle as I brush over her. She arches under my touch. I don't press against the skin, only lightly brush my fingers over her a few times before spreading her and doing the same over her swollen clit. "Oh, you poor thing. You really need some kisses, don't you?" I bring my hands back and Lia frowns at me. Her frown deepens when I pick up her coffee and take a drink, sucking one of the ice cubes into my mouth. I hold it against my tongue and then spread her again. I let the ice touch her burning skin.

"Oh," her voice is hardly more than a puff of breath. I work the ice over her, careful not to leave it in one spot for too long. I let the ice melt against the tip of my tongue so I know I'm nice and cold for her, and then I let my tongue ease her tenderness. I lap at her entrance and her clit. I taste and kiss every inch of her pussy with my chilled lips and look up to find Aren watching intently, his hand moving through her hair and massaging her scalp. He holds her wrists in his other hand, but his hold is gentle. Her head is back, her eyes closed, and her mouth parts on a silent moan.

I pull away once more to get another ice cube and then I start all over again. Once this cube is melted, and my tongue is warm after being inside her, I curl a single finger inside her and suck hard at her clit. That's all it takes for her back to arch off the bed and her pussy to clench around my finger. I spread another round of soft kisses over her slick skin and then Aren releases her wrists and helps her sit up. I lean over to steal another ice cube, and this time I hold it and run it over her lips and then down her neck. I find every single mark Aren left on her and I press the ice there before licking away the melted water. When I'm done, I give her a few slow kisses and then crawl back into bed next to her. "Did I miss anywhere?" I ask against her ear.

She can only shake her head, looking sleepy again. "Eat up, Sunshine." Then I look up at Aren who is still watching us with a dark gaze. "How was that, Daddy?"

"Seriously, what the actual fuck? Stop calling me that!"

"Don't listen to him, he likes it." Lia finally says, eyeing her coffee with a small frown. I drank quite a bit of it to get the ice I needed. Aren sees this and gets up, offering to get this round since he ate his food while I ate Lia. She rests her head on my shoulder and the two of us finish our breakfast with a quiet, sleepy ease between us.

21

LIA

Mara eyes me with a small frown as we sit around a table to figure out the best way to go after Vram and whatever men he's retained. I just want a nap. I still feel drained from my activities with Aren the night before, and even Enzo's gentleness this morning has taken what little energy I had. I'm absolutely blissed out, and I just want to enjoy it under a pile of covers on a comfy mattress. Both of my men have kept their hands to themselves and been nothing but professional since we got to Zane and Mara's house, but I can physically feel each of their gazes when their eyes stray to me. It's not lost on me that their bodies stay turned towards me and adjust when I move. I'm as aware of them as they are of me. I'm also very aware of the fact that Mara is seeing all of this and connecting the dots. I'm not sure either of us are paying any attention to what the men are suggesting. I'm too busy trying to hide what is happening, and Mara is too busy seeing it, anyway. We are being terrible women in power right now. We should be ashamed.

"I'm going to take Ani out. Lia, come with me." Mara says, standing and abruptly stopping the talk.

"Everything okay?" Zane touches the small of her back, his brows pulled down in worry as he eyes her.

"Yup. I just need to stretch my legs. We'll be back." She doesn't leave room for me to argue and I glance between my men. We all know we are busted. I can feel their questions as I stand and follow my cousin outside.

"Okay, what is all that energy in there?" She turns on me the second the glass door shuts behind us. Ani takes off at a run the moment Mara picks up a tennis ball. She chucks it across the courtyard.

"Well..." I'm not ashamed of what we have, but it's also hard to explain. Mara has always seen both Aren and I as her cousins. She accepted me as family the moment my mother married into it. While our feelings have never been quite familial, Aren and I are step siblings. And then when you add Enzo to the mix... we aren't exactly a traditional bunch.

"Lia." Mara takes my hands in hers. "I'm here, okay? I can tell something is going on, I'm just not sure what it is. I promise I won't judge whatever it is, and I promise I'm on your side."

I take a deep breath. "The three of us... have decided to," I shake my head, "date, I guess."

Mara grins widely before pulling me into a hug that takes me by surprise. She's always allowed me to hug her, she's taken it in stride, but she's never been one to initiate touch. After everything she's been through it's completely understandable, but now she's the one pulling me into a tight squeeze. "I can't believe it! I mean, I can. The way the two of them have been looking at you. But," she releases me, "wow!"

"You... you're okay with all this? I mean Aren and I-"

"Oh please. You guys were practically adults when your parents got married, and he's always been extra possessive about you. It went beyond protective and I always thought it went far beyond brotherly feelings. I'm more surprised that he'd let Enzo anywhere near you."

"Well, he didn't have much of a choice."

"Way to go, Lia!" Something flashes across Mara's face and her smile falls just a fraction.

"What?" I ask, suddenly weary.

Her gaze darts to the house and she gives herself a minute to think through what she wants to say by grabbing the ball from Ani's mouth and giving it another toss across the yard. I watch Ani zoom after it and do my best to give Mara the space to figure out her words. "Okay," she sighs heavily. "I'm not sure if you know this already, or if I should be the one to say anything, but I feel like you should know. Enzo joined Zane and I in the bedroom once. It was only once, and it didn't mean anything. Well," she rambles, "it meant something to me because it was like Zane was giving me control over myself and my choices. He gave me room to explore and didn't judge or anything like that. It helped me to realize I had fallen in love with him. But Enzo was his best friend and the only person he would have trusted. And it's probably not even something he's even thought of as an issue, but I feel like..." Mara looks at me, her eyes wide with worry. "I would feel weird about not telling you. I wouldn't want you to think I was hiding it or anything."

"Oh." I take in the information and let it settle. It is odd that Enzo didn't tell me, but I also know that he enjoys sharing, and if Zane was willing to let Enzo join him and Mara, I'd assume they've shared before. For Enzo, it probably was just another night of fun and isn't something he really sees as an issue. Mara clearly doesn't see it as an issue, and while it's weird that we've technically shared a dick now, I think my life has a lot of other weird going on for this to really be a problem. "So, sex with Enzo made you realize you loved Zane?" I tease, wrapping my arm around her shoulder to show we are okay.

"Yeah, I guess so. Is that weird?"

"Listen, who am I to judge?" I press a loud kiss to her cheek and take the ball from Ani this time, doing my best to ignore the slobber. "So, you're okay with all this, then?" I ask once more.

"Of course; it's badass! I love this for you. And even if I didn't, you've got to worry about your own happiness. It's your life at the end of the day, and you've only got one of those."

"Are you happy?"

"Yes," Mara's smile is huge. "Most of my life, I was just surviving. I just needed to get to the next day and then the next day. But now I feel like I'm actually who I was always meant to be. Zane is great, and I love him so much, but it's also really nice to just feel secure in my skin for once."

"Good, you deserve it. Now we just have to get rid of our little problem and we can all ride into the sunset."

"Yeah, what's life without a little murder and mayhem?"

"It's not easy being badass, but someone has to do it." We bump shoulders. "Nothing we can't handle. I guess we should head back in and actually help the men plan our attack." Mara agrees and calls Ani back over to her. We walk arm in arm back to the room where the men respectfully took a break from their plans until our return. Zane eyes his wife carefully before flicking to me, clearly trying to assess the situation. Mara releases me and goes to him, kissing his cheek before pushing him down onto his chair so she can sit in his lap. She flashes me a grin when his hands quickly go to her middle to pull her back against him securely without a single argument to the seating arrangement. I take up the seat between my men once more and ignore their silent questions. Enzo reaches under the table and gives my leg a little squeeze. When I look at him, I find a worried question there and wonder if he knows what Mara told me. If he's just realizing that maybe I would care that he once slept with my cousin. I reach for his hand and thread my fingers through his.

"Okay, what plan will keep my shoes clean? Because I gotta say, I'm not for getting messy."

"Well, that's just not accura-"

"Enzo, shut the fuck up." Aren demands dully. Mara chuckles under her breath and I glare at Enzo.

"I haven't heard of any issues or threats from any of my contacts." Aren starts. "Our businesses have been secured and watched carefully, and there have been no signs of threats. The attacks seemed focused on the Moretti properties, which makes sense with it being Vram. If his goal is to take it from us, he's probably a little more willing to damage the Moretti side since he doesn't have as much information on them. He'd have all the information on Papazian businesses because of Hayk."

"There are no sides, not anymore." Zane grumbles, pulling Mara closer.

"We may be one big happy family now, but on the streets, there are still sides. On the streets, it's still Moretti and Papazian land and we are just allies. So, I can see them focusing on the Moretti territory. They don't know that we've combined everything behind the scenes too." Enzo leans back as he talks, at ease with everyone at the table and back to business even after teasing me. "So we should focus our efforts in watching more of the Moretti territory. If we can get eyes on one of the lackeys, we might be able to follow them back to daddy." The tiniest lift at the corner of Enzo's mouth tells me he did that on purpose. Aren stiffens next to me, sending a glare that goes right through me to Enzo.

"I'd like to have a way to be on the offense with this though." Mara speaks up, straightening her back.

"I'll get some of our hackers looking into it. Maybe we can find a money trail or communication. Now that we know more of what we are looking for and from whom, we have a better chance of catching something. If we can trace it to where he is, we can call in our guns and even our allies and take care of this mess once and for all." Zane seems to forget the rest of us are here as he trails his lips down Mara's neck. The sight of the small touch sends heat down my spine, making me wish for touch. The soreness between my legs flares alive as a deep ache for my men begins. I shift in my seat, doing what I can to cut off the random naughty thoughts. I've gone basically my whole life without any relief that wasn't given by my own hand, and now I have two men driving me crazy. It seems very unfair that I can't just spend a week in bed with them to soak in it.

"So, it seems like we have next steps. We can stop by a few places on our way home and I'll check in with our men on how everything has been looking. I want to make sure our people are protected as much as they can be." Enzo's hand moves farther up my thigh as he talks, and then suddenly Aren's hand is on my other thigh. I glance between them, trying to figure out if they are aware of the other. When they both gently tug my legs apart, I figure they've somehow learned to communicate silently, because of course they would.

"Sounds good. Keep in touch, and I'll update if anything new comes through." Zane basically dismisses everyone, and when I catch his hand trailing under the table, I have a good idea of why he might want some privacy. Both hands leave me and the three of us stand almost in unison.

Mara leaves her husband's lap to pull me into a hug and I'm again surprised by her initiation of affection. I squeeze her back, and after everyone says goodbye, Enzo takes my hand to lead me out of the house. Aren leads the way, but when Enzo goes to open the passenger door, Aren grabs my other hand and tugs me to the backseat. He says nothing, but when I climb in, he climbs in after me, shutting the door in Enzo's face. Enzo rolls his eyes but walks back around the car to take up the driver's seat.

"Let's have some fun, shall we?" Enzo turns to shoot me a wink, and then revs the engine.

22

Aren

Feeling Lia pressed against me is pure torture. I don't plan on suffering though; I plan on doing something about it. I kiss her first, touching the soft skin of her neck, nipping at her jaw, before I finally turn her head so I can taste her lips. She moans so easily for me as Enzo speeds down the road.

"Don't you dare fucking crash." I groan as I undo her seatbelt and pull her so she's sitting on my lap. Enzo responds with a curse, but Lia grins, her eyes bright with mirth as she sits down against my thighs. I wrap her long blond hair around my fist and pull back, exposing her throat. I squeeze the tender skin and feel her breath catch even as she rubs against me, wanting more. "You think you can take me, Lia? You think you can ride me?"

She nods, her eyes on me as she presses against my cock. I just shake my head. She's so eager to please, even though I'm sure she's still a little sore from my taking her for so long last night. I lift her to rip away her clothes and thank Enzo silently for his darkened windows. "Aren, please." Her nimble fingers go to my zipper and she works it down while I flick the button open. She takes me in her hand, rubbing my tip but waiting for me to tell her what to do next. I slap the side of her breast just enough to draw her attention away from my cock for a moment. Her eyes flash to mine and I grin and do it again, a little harder this time, so that the sound of the slap rings in the car. Whatever music had been playing is off now, probably so Enzo can hear us better.

"Look at how red your skin gets. And how easily you hold the marks I left on your skin. You are a piece of artwork."

She leans forward to draw me into another kiss, but I grab her by the throat again, squeezing gently to test how much she likes. She doesn't pull away. Instead, her eyes roll back in pleasure, and her thighs squeeze against my legs, trying to find some friction. "I asked if you could fucking ride me, baby. Why are you just stroking me like some doll? Take what you need. Be my little slut and show me how needy you are."

Enzo curses from the front seat, but continues to drive with ease, so I know he's still keeping us safe. It's amazing that Lia can let go like this with me while the car is moving. And it's a fucking miracle that I'm trusting him like this. All my attention is on Lia, and I'm leaving our lives in his hands and driving abilities. Lia leans into my hand, so I squeeze a little harder and watch as she lines my dick up with her center. I keep one hand on her neck, but I steady her hips with my other hand as she lowers herself and breathes out at the stretch of me entering her. Then her hands are on my shoulders and she rides. I have to release her neck so I can fully hold on to her as she bounces on my dick, her head bent forward so she doesn't hit the top of the car. The wet sounds of our bodies coming together is addicting and I can't help but groan at the feel of her slickness and warmth around me.

"Aren," she pants my name, and that has me thrusting my hips to meet hers. I know I hit her deep inside from the way her breathing changes. She bites her lip so hard I think she might make it bleed, but if she does, I'll clean the blood away with my tongue. Everything about her is mine. Mine. The car stops, but I'm too enthralled with Lia to know if we are at our first destination, or if we are stuck at a light. Fuck, a cop can pull us over right now, and there is no way I'm going to stop fucking this woman. She'd look hot in the cuffs, and the idea of making her come in the back of a police car has me gripping her hips harder. She cries out and goes still as her pussy throbs around me, squeezing out my own orgasm as she shakes. When she looks at me, there are tears in her eyes.

"Now that's a good girl. Being my good little slut." I wipe the tears away, wishing I was someone who could be softer with her. I wish I could be a little less possessive, a bit more gentle. But she can have Enzo for that. I want her raw and shaking. I need the tears and the marks on her skin that show her as mine. I fought taking her for so many years, but she gave herself over to me, and now she'll have to pay the consequences. With a deep breath, I pull her against my chest, her naked skin damp against my clothes. I brush her hair back and wipe away the tears that spilled over. "Did you take what you needed?" I ask.

Her smile wobbles, but then brightens as she nods her head. "For now. But I believe we are going to make the back of Enzo's car messy."

"Fuck the car. Move off of him slowly, Sunshine. I want to see just how messy you are as it drips down your legs." Enzo joins in and I slowly realize we are parked. So we must be at one of the businesses he wanted to take us to. Lia moves her body off of me slowly, sticking her ass up in the air as she does. My gaze goes to the sight of her as she lifts away from me and tracks of our pleasure start down her thighs.

"You should clean her up. Can't have her walking around like that." I order; my eyes leave her and go to Enzo. He doesn't take his gaze from her, but grins at my words. Then he leaves the car to come to the back door, and I look around. We are in a parking garage, and no one seems to be around. That's not a guarantee we won't get caught, but fuck it. Who would dare to say something to us? I pull her against me, kissing her neck when she rests against my chest while my back leans against the opposite door. Enzo opens the one in front of us and sticks the top half of his body in; and then wraps her legs around his head. Lia whimpers when his tongue laps at the wetness between her thighs. But she arches against me when he finds her center and really gets to work cleaning her up. It's not long before she's shaking again, crushed between us as he devours. I tweak her nipple when it feels like she's getting close to another peak. Without even communicating, Enzo senses the same thing and shoves two of his fingers inside her at the same time, tipping her over. He spends a little more time there, finishing the job of cleaning her. When he pulls away, he's grinning like he just had the time of his life, his lips glistening with the mixture of Lia and I.

"Fuck," Lia whispers, collapsing against me with a shaky laugh. "I'm not going anywhere. I'm going to stay here and nap."

"But they have coffee. And chocolatey baked goods." Enzo teases, wiping his mouth and moving so his body blocks the doorway. He leans down and grabs her clothes from the floor of the car and starts redressing her. Maybe Lia does need both of us. I want to care for her and take care of her, but I tend to do it by making sure no threats come near her while he seems to do the little things for her naturally. Things she's perfectly capable of doing for herself, but that she seems to enjoy letting him do. Lia pulls away from me so he can hook her bra and pull her dress back over her head. Then he grins and shakes his head. "There's nothing we can do about your hair. It's a lost cause. We might just have to cut it off."

"No, you fucking won't. I enjoy pulling on it." I growl, catching her around the middle and pulling her back onto my lap so I can wrap that hair around my fist again. Her little moan warms all the cold places inside of me, so I reward her with a soft kiss to her cheek. "Come on, baby." I scoot out of the backseat with her on my lap and make sure she has her balance standing before I follow her out. "You need a bigger car. My knees don't have room in this one."

Enzo just chuckles and takes Lia's hand in his own. "Come on, I promised caffeine and chocolate."

We visit two small shops that the Moretti family uses as covers, and Enzo greets everyone by name. He checks in with his people while I follow Lia so she can order drinks and snacks. It's not until we enter a gun shop that Enzo hears of anything suspicious.

Apparently, there was an attempted break-in two days before. The person didn't get in so they hadn't reached out, just replaced the damaged door and moved on, thinking it was probably a random attempt. Enzo sends a message to Zane and then drives us to the last stop of the day. Lia seems to be wearing down, the click of her heels slower as she drags behind me a bit.

"You okay?" I ask, stopping so she can catch up. It's just a pawn shop, but normally I'd expect Lia to explore more, looking for that something special hidden away on a shelf somewhere.

"I'm jello. I don't think I can handle two men." She shakes her head seriously. "You guys might have to trade off weeks or something. Maybe you can act like divorced parents and drop me off for the weekend or-"

"That would not go how you think it would. If we didn't have easy access to you, that would just mean we'd never let you leave the bed when it was our turn. Plus," I step right up against her so she has to tilt her head to meet my gaze. "We know you enjoy having us both. You'd miss whoever wasn't around."

She sighs heavily, her shoulders lifting with exaggeration. "Fine. But I demand a hot bath when we get home. And a glass of wine. And maybe one of you can massage my feet while the other does my shoulders. I want to be a pampered princess." She juts out her lip in a pout that is way too adorable for a grown woman. A fucking sexy woman.

"Agreed. But the next time we share you," I bend down to brush my lips against her ear, "I'm taking your ass while you ride Enzo. And I plan on taking my time." The filthy promise gives her a lovely blush across her cheeks.

Enzo joins us again. "Leave her alone. The woman needs some rest." He chides when he takes in the pretty pink across her cheeks.

"I wasn't doing anything. Just telling her what I want in exchange for treating her like a princess tonight. She wants massages and a bath."

"And wine."

"See? She's very needy." I tease.

"Wow, Lia. You really wanted this grump? I thought that Daddy Dom was supposed to be nice after fucking your brains out?"

"Seriously, what the fuck is up with the daddy dom bit?"

23

ENZO

"I've planned a night out for all of us." Aren is frowning at his laptop and Lia is sleeping in after being pampered last night. She slept right through both of us getting out of bed this morning, and as much as I'm sure she needs the rest, it also feels strange to leave her in that big bed alone. It feels wrong, like at least one of us should have stayed in there with her. But I wanted to follow up with Zane about the attempted break-in at the weapons shop and see if there is anywhere else he thinks I should make a priority to check in with today. Aren apparently doesn't know how to sleep in. He was up before me and was already a coffee in before I met up with him.

"Okay?" He shrugs, not bothering to look up.

Man of many words, as usual. I decide to just finish my breakfast and wait to tell Lia about it instead. If she goes, Aren is sure to follow. His phone rings so he stands to take it in the other room and I finish my coffee just as Lia walks in. She combed her hair and probably brushed her teeth, but she's fresh from bed otherwise. Her smile is sleepy and her shorts are deliciously short. "Morning, Sunshine."

"You both left me." She pouts.

"You slept too long. We tried to wake you. Aren was between

your legs, doing all he could to kiss you awake. But you just snored right along. It got boring, so we came down for a proper breakfast instead."

"He did not!"

"Okay, fine. He didn't, as far as I know. He was up before I was." I cradle her face and kiss her gently. "If it makes you feel any better, it felt strange leaving you in an empty bed. When you have two men at your beck and call, I feel like you should always wake up curled up against at least one of us."

"I agree. In the future, it doesn't matter if I stay in bed all day long. As long as I'm in there, at least one of you has to stay with me."

"This feels like a hostage situation."

"Well, you've seen me use a blade. You've been warned." She grins and then leaves the cradle of my arms to fix herself a plate. "So, should we talk about this whole living situation? Are Aren and I moving in here officially? We still have the Papazian side of things to monitor. Should we go back? Drag you with us?"

"We should probably discuss it when Aren is in the room. But I don't see why we can't just hop between both houses. There's no way in hell I'm letting you run off without me. But we can certainly take up shop at your place and come back here when we need to. I don't want anything to get overlooked. Or we can just take trips as needed." I sit beside her at the table and get all warm and fuzzy at the idea of her thinking about our group living situation.

"Okay." She grins at me, her whole face lighting up. "It feels strange to be this happy."

"Why do you say that?"

"I don't know. There's always been a huge looming shadow of danger. And there still is, but right now, I'm not worried about what might come. I'm just happy. I have two men to pamper me and now two houses to fill with all of my shoes."

"What on earth have the two of you been talking about while I was out of the room?"

Aren speaks up from the doorway, frowning in our direction.

"Do not give her any excuse to get more shoes. Please, you don't understand the ability our woman has for collecting shoes."

"Hey Aren," Lia smiles sweetly. "I love you, but shut the fuck up. Don't mess this up for me."

"I'm sorry, did you just declare your love for him?" I pout. "And then follow it up by telling him to shut the fuck up?"

"Yes! He's going to warn you about my shoe addiction, and that's just not cool. You should have the opportunity to find this out for yourself. And by then, I plan on having you wrapped around my finger so that you don't even notice." She looks between us, seeming to realize that we are both staring at her silently. Then she rolls her eyes and tosses her hair to the side. "Fucking boys, the both of you. Aren, I love you. I'm in love with you. Suck it up and stop looking like you swallowed a lemon." Then she turns on me, anger lighting up her cheeks. "And I'm also in love with you, you fucking idiot. Obviously I love the both of you, or I wouldn't let you do all the very dirty things the two of you have been doing to me."

"Oh, you haven't seen dirty yet, Sunshine." I stroke her cheek. "We've hardly even played with you together yet. And, just so it's on the record, I love you, too. Also, you already have me wrapped around your finger, and I don't need a lot of closet space, so I don't really mind the shoes. We all have our vices." I kiss her lips softly to seal our declaration. Aren steps up behind her and I know he presses against her because her body pushes flush against me. His hands move down her sides until they come to rest on her hips. Her eyes glitter when his lips move down her cheek to kiss under her jaw.

"I love you, Lia. We are in this together, shoe addiction and all."

"Good, because I love you both, but I might love my shoes more." She sighs, sandwiched happily between us.

"I thought we could take you out to dinner tonight, but maybe I should just take you shoe shopping instead." I eye her.

"I'll go to dinner, but I am not going shoe shopping." Aren groans. "I've done my time. I have years of shopping with you under my belt. You can take your other boyfriend for that for a few years and then maybe we can swap again."

"Oh, come on, Daddy Dom. Don't you want to reward me for being such a good girl?" Lia turns to look at Aren over her shoulder. He just glares down at her.

"For the rare occasion you are, in fact, a good girl, I have other ways to reward you."

"I don't know if I want other ways. I just want shoes." The sound of Aren's hand slapping her ass echoes in the room and I chuckle as her cheeks go bright red. I'd love to see if her ass cheek matches the same red tint, but I know that I have some things to get done today, so I take a step back from them.

"Okay, well, I'll let the two of you argue about this. But I am going to stop by a few places today and then follow up with Zane. Then I'll take the two of you to dinner."

"Oh, I actually need to take a drive to one of the Papazian businesses." Lia and I both look to Aren at that. "Everything is okay, but our people have been keeping an ear to the ground and they think they might have a lead. I just got off the phone with them and told them I'd head there to see if we can uncover anything." He eyes Lia. "You can come with me, but I don't know that I'll get back with a lot of time for you to get ready for the date."

Lia rolls her eyes. "It's fine. I don't need a sitter! Enzo has guards posted and I can just stay here."

Aren meets my gaze in a silent question. I don't really like leaving her here alone, even with guards posted, but I'm sure she could also use a bit of time on her own. She's had the two of us around for weeks now. One of us has always been with her. I give the slightest nod that she'll be safe enough, so Aren agrees. He turns her in his arms so he can give her a solid kiss, his hand cupping her jaw and tilting her face up to his. "Be safe then. I'll see you tonight. I'll message you both how everything is going on my end."

"I shouldn't be too long. I can always come pick you up before I go to Zane if you want to stop and see Mara?"

"Maybe. Text me when you think you are about to head over and I'll let you know how I'm feeling then?"

I agree and kiss her too, giving her ass a nice little squeeze for my own enjoyment. She swats my hand playfully, but she's grinning ear to ear when she does. "Have fun, boys. I'm going to go enjoy some peace and quiet." She turns her back on us both and gives us a delightful view of the sway of her hips as she goes down the hall, the click of her heels going straight to my balls. Damnit.

"Go ahead, you have a drive ahead of you. I'll talk to the guards before I go and I'll have them send us updates every half hour."

Aren gives me a nod of agreement, grabs a coffee to go, and then heads out.

24

LIA

I spend a good portion of my day just relaxing. The men took good care of me last night, but it also feels nice to have the place to myself for once. I love them, and I miss them, but I hardly ever get time alone. I blast pop music and scroll social media like it's my job. Then I decide to start choosing my look for the evening. The idea of going on a date with both of my men makes me all hot and bothered, so I want to make sure they spend the evening hot and bothered looking at me. I take my time to make sure I'm shaved and smooth. I put some nice bouncy curls in my hair and do my make-up with a nice shadowed eye and bright red lipstick to match the form-fitting red dress I chose for the evening. I choose strappy lingerie with a corset top I know will make their mouths water when they see it. And I certainly expect to end the night with them seeing it.

Enzo messages me when he's heading over to Zane's but I'm having fun primping, so I choose to stay. The guards mostly stay outside, but one of them comes to check on me here and there, wanting to get eyes on me before I assume they send my men an update on my well-being. I'm putting on extra high heels when there is a loud noise outside. I step out into the hall, expecting to see one of the guards after letting the door slam by mistake, but the house is empty. The feeling of wrongness hits me dead center. I take a step back, planning to go back to my room to call Enzo, but the distinct sound of gunshots freezes me in place. My heart slams against my chest and then, finally, my feet move. I rush back into my room, slamming my door shut behind me and locking it. I have no idea who is outside, or what their plan is, but I'm not expecting it to be good. I grab my phone and hit Enzo's name. Aren is too far away, but Enzo can bring Zane and be here in minutes.

"Hello, Sunshine." His deep voice is flirty as he answers.

"Enzo! There are gunshots!"

"What the fuck? Tell me what exactly is happening. Where are you?" I hear him moving and yelling for Zane, already on the move to stop whatever this is.

"I'm in my room. The door is locked. I heard a loud noise and now there are gunshots. That's all I know. I don't think anyone is inside, but the front door was unlocked, the guards have been stepping in to check on me all day."

"We are coming." I hear the start of an engine and the sound floods me with relief. "Just stay on the phone with me, but stay quiet, okay? Find somewhere to hide, just in case they get past the guards."

I nod even though he can't see me and look around my room. I don't have a weapon in here, but I go to the closet and grab one of my pointiest heels and then crouch down behind some of my dresses. "Good girl, just stay quiet. Zane is driving and we are coming for you."

There's another loud crash, and then men yelling back and forth to one another. "They are inside." I whisper. Shit. I should have just gone with Enzo. I should have gone with Aren. I should have been active in all of this today instead of hiding away for some time alone. I realize I'm shaking and I must be breathing harder because Enzo whispers reassurances, though his voice sounds a little tighter than usual. I hear him growl for Zane to drive faster when my bedroom door crashes open. I cover my mouth to stop myself from crying out at the sound.

"Search the other rooms. The men should be out; it should

just be the bitch."

"We are coming, Lia. We are almost there." Enzo tells me, but I can hardly hear him over the pounding of my heart. I ready the heel in my hand as I hear the man walk around my room. I put my phone down my dress and between my breasts, tucked tight in the corset. I can't hear Enzo now, but he will hopefully still be able to hear me, and I need both of my hands if I have to fight. The sound of my bathroom door slamming into a wall makes me want to cry, but I focus on taking deep breaths. I killed the last man that tried to take me. I'm not about to go down without a fight this time around.

The man kicks in the closet door next and I back up as much as I can, pressing my back flat against the wall. If I can keep him from seeing me, that's my best option, but once he sees me, I won't have the advantage to attack. I see the hand reaching out to move the clothes aside, and I know I'm about to be found. So I spring to my feet and throw myself at him. He falls back with a grunt as I crash against his large, solid body. I bring my heel back and slam it with all of my strength into his head.

"Fuck!" He reaches out to grab me, but I move out of the way and swing back to hit him again, aiming for his eye this time. He dodges at the last second, so instead of taking out his eye, my heel breaks the skin on his cheek. The man growls at me, and this time, he makes sure I can't dodge. He throws his body at me and we both crash to the floor. His hands find my wrists and he slams them hard on the ground over and over until I finally release the heel. "Fucking bitch!" He stands and drags me up with him. I go limp in his arms, a dead weight for him to stand up with, but the man is built like a truck and continues to move with ease.

"Short beard, brown eyes, short curly brown hair." I scream out his description the moment I truly see him. "A nice fucking cut down his cheek."

He slaps me to cut off my words. "Shut the fuck up. Are there cameras in here?" He looks up and around the room as he drags me from the closet. "Good, we want them to see as we take you. We might not be able to get to the Papazian queen just yet, but you are a good start." He releases me for just a second, but only to let go of my wrists and grab my hair instead. The pain in my scalp makes me want to cry out, but I know Enzo can hear what's happening. He's on his way to me; I just need to buy them some time. So I thrash. I throw my body around even as strands of hair rip from my scalp in his fist. He kicks my leg so that I fall to my knees and drags me across the floor of my room. I know there are cameras in here. Enzo keeps them off, but I'm sure he's been able to turn them on since I called him. If he doesn't get here in time, I certainly want him and Aren to know I fought. I want them to see me draw blood of my own. So I reach up and find the arm holding my hair. I scratch my nails down the skin that I find and take pleasure at the sound of him cursing.

"I've got her!" He yells out and seconds later three other men join us in the room. "She's a fucking psycho." The man pushes me to the ground and I don't catch myself in time. My face slams to the floor, but I scramble back from the boots approaching me.

"She's fucking hot. Maybe the boss will let us play with her once we get her out of here." One of the new men sneers.

"Fuck. You." I hold up my middle finger, but it seems they're done playing with me now. The tears finally well in my eyes as they circle me. Enzo has to be close. It feels like this has been going on for hours. He has to get here in time.

"Maybe you'll get the chance." The man that found me crouches down to grin at me with his disgusting promise. I grin back at him and fall back on my ass. He only has a second to frown at me, wondering why I just fell over, before I kick out my foot and hit him right in the balls with my heeled foot. I don't get the pleasure of watching him suffer though, because whoever is behind me grabs me, and then my head explodes in pain and darkness takes me. But I take the sound of a man crying with me.

25

Enzo

"Zane," I stare at my phone screen and watch the fight happening. Zane is already breaking all the laws to get us through traffic and to my house before these assholes have the chance to leave with the woman I love. Lia won't go down without a fight, but they're hurting her. I can hear the fight through the speaker, muffled as it is after she shoved her phone down her shirt. It was a smart move; my girl is fucking bright, and she's a fighter. Weaponless and outnumbered, she doesn't go down easily.

"Fuck!" I slam my fist against the car as I watch one of them hit her in the back of her head with the butt of a gun. She goes limp, and the man picks her up. I look up and see we are still two blocks away. The men move quickly once she's down. I watch them through the cameras as they leave the house, and I know we will not get there in time. I switch to the outside cameras, ignoring the sight of the guards dead on the ground, and focus on the cars instead. There's two of them, both of them dark gray Hondas. They want to get out and get lost in traffic. I tell Zane the cars we are looking for just as they pull out and disappear from the cameras. "West, they turned west."

"Shit." Zane grumbles as he swerves around cars stopped at a red light. He hits the gas and narrowly avoids getting us T-boned.

The muffled sound of Lia in the car is still coming through the speakers, so they haven't found her phone yet. I close the cameras and pull up the tracker on her phone before putting the map on the dashboard so Zane can follow the line. Without us speaking, Zane hands me his phone so I can keep working while he drives. I call Romano, knowing he can reach out to the rest of our guns. "We are following a lead to Vram. They have Lia. I'm sending you her location." I hang up without waiting for a response, trusting Romano to get the work done. Then I dial Aren.

"My leads didn't go anywhere." Aren starts speaking as soon as he answers. "Enzo made us dinner plans, but I can stop over tomorrow to give you all of the-"

"It's me." I interrupt. "Men came to the house, and they took Lia. I'm with Zane and we are in pursuit."

"Excuse me?" He thunders just as I hear the engine of his car rev as he picks up speed.

"They killed the guards and grabbed her. She still has her phone with her, so we are tracking it. We already sent in the order for everyone to follow. I'm going to send it to you and you can head straight there. She's okay; they knocked her out, but probably only because she was determined to take them all down with nothing but her heels and nails. I'm still on a call with her so I can hear what's happening. We are getting her back."

"Fuck! Fuck!" I hear him slam his hands on the steering wheel. "Fine. Send me the location. I'm twenty minutes out from home, but I'll get to you as soon as I can." He hangs up on me so I can send the information. He's definitely going to punch me in the face the next time we are in the same space.

"Do you think they are taking her right to Vram?"

"If we are lucky." Zane answers, his knuckles white on the steering wheel.

My knee bounces as we drive and I just keep watching the dot that is Lia as it moves through the map. As long as she can keep that phone on, we are okay. I try to pay attention to everything around her as her dot continues to move, just in case it drops out. I can't think of anywhere good for them to be set up from where they are, but the car doesn't show signs of stopping just yet. All I can hear through her phone is the light rustle of her clothes against the phone. If the men in the car with her are talking, they are doing so quietly. I turn up the volume just in case I can pick out anything else happening. We can't seem to gain speed on them and continue to trail behind, which makes me feel sick. I can't believe these men found where I was, got in, and managed to get my girl. They seemed to know Aren and I were out of the house, which makes me wonder if Aren's lead was just a lark to lead him away. They couldn't have known Lia would get left alone, but they could have taken the chance or even just hoped to lower our numbers to make it easier to get to her. Whatever their plan, it worked out well enough for them for the time being; but we are coming, and we are bringing our army. I can only hope that they are leading us to the head so we can chop it the fuck off.

26

LIA

I wake with a pounding headache and the feeling of my legs being asleep. I blink slowly and find myself tied to a pipe in the wall, my ass planted on the hard, cold floor of some hide-away. They got me out of the house. I seem to be alone at the moment, so I wiggle my body so I can try to squish my boobs together to feel if my phone is still there. I feel exposed in a way I didn't before when I realize it's gone. Did it fall out? Or did one of those men reach into my dress and lingerie to get it? Losing the phone also makes me feel alone. I have no idea when the phone was lost. Does Enzo know where I am? He won't have a way to track me if I don't have the phone. How much did he hear? Was he able to watch them on the cameras? I start to spiral when the door bangs open and the group of men saunter in, minus the one I scratched and kicked in the groin. I hope I kicked him hard enough to rupture his balls with my heel.

"Well, look who woke up. I worried I hit your head a little too hard. It was nice of you to get so dressed up for us though." The man lets his beady little eyes wander the length of my body curled on the floor.

"If you had let me know you were coming ahead of time, I

could have added some fun accessories. I have plenty of shiny daggers I think you would just love."

"I think your phone was enough of a happy surprise. Donny here took great pleasure doing a body search. I hope you didn't have anything important saved on it since it's smashed on the side of the road somewhere."

All I can do is glare and hope they didn't find it until we were close to our location, or they said where we were going so that Enzo overheard it. "Ah," another man enters and this one clearly thinks he's in charge. His grey suit is expensive, his hair styled, and his grin is lecherous. "Our beautiful hostage." He looks me over slowly. "I can see why you've been so protected over the years. You and Tamara have been the forbidden fruit left to tempt all the men. My cousin was promised one, but," he tuts and shakes his head slowly. "Guess he didn't get her, did he? Now she's been all dirtied up with that Moretti scum. But you," he crouches down and tucks a finger under my chin. I pull back as far as I can, my skin crawling from his touch. This just amuses him more. His eyes take me in and for the first time in my life, I regret my outfit choice. My men are coming for me. As much as I hate the idea of being a damsel in distress, I'll enjoy watching Enzo and Aren rip this guy and the other men to shreds for me. The thought makes me grin. I tilt my chin up and let all my wicked ideas play havoc on my features.

"What do you want with me?"

"I plan on putting you up for sale. Don't worry, I'll invite Zane Moretti. He'll have his chance to bid for you. But while they are scrambling for you, I'm bringing the war down on their heads. They already pulled their resources to come after you. A good idea when they were so close to getting to you. But," he sucks on his teeth, "unfortunately they lost their signal. Their people are running around with no destination, and my people are going for all of their businesses. I heard you were at the little club when it was attacked. But that was just one." He stands and wipes at his pant legs like being close to the ground I'm on was enough to soil his clothing. He leaves me without a backwards glance and takes my hope with him.

They lost the signal too soon and they have no way to find me. Not until he's ready for them to.

A man releases my hands and pulls me to my feet. Pins and needles break out across my body, making me cry out as I roll my ankle in my heels, unable to feel it more than the burst of pain that flares. "Hold her steady; I want some good pics. Don't worry, doll. You get to keep your clothes on for these. The really fun ones will come later." The man is older than the rest, with stained teeth and a rough voice that makes me think he's spent most of his life as a smoker. He raises a camera, and the flash makes me feel sick. Oh, fuck this. I try to pull free from the hands holding me, but he just chuckles and holds me tight enough to bruise my skin.

"Make sure I'm in the room for the pics you take later. I'd love to see what's under this dress." His hand moves to squeeze at my waist. I jerk my elbow back and hit him in the stomach. His hand goes back to pin my arms, but I take my little win.

"You know, I'm pretty sure they make a pill for small dick syndrome now. Maybe you should look into that." I spit out the words when the cameraman leaves and the man holding me down drags me from the room. I barely keep up with my heels, but I do my best. He opens the door to another room with a very questionable mattress on the floor and a chain hanging from the wall. A new man stands there but is busy doing something on his phone. I hardly see him, I just see the mattress and feel the sickness rising in my throat.

"You should learn to keep your fucking mouth shut before I show you just how large my cock is when I shove it down your throat."

"If you tried, I'd bite it off and shove it up your own ass."

The man glances up from his phone and chuckles. "She's fun. Maybe we should keep her around for entertainment."

"Maybe she should realize she's not in control here." The man growls, slapping my face before shoving me down onto the mattress. Fear clutches me. I don't want them to touch me, but I will not back down. I can't. It's all I have right now.

"I will not make myself smaller to make you feel like a big

strong man. You are already dead, you just don't know it yet. The moment you so much as looked in my direction, you wrote your own death warrant. They are already coming for you and they are bringing a fucking army. You chose a side, and you chose the wrong damn one." I grin, ignoring the pull of my bloody lip. "I hope they make your death last for days."

"I hope the boss kills you, cuts you up, and hangs all your parts outside so they see that when they first get here. Then we can just gun them down like stunned little rats. Every single one of them."

"Maybe you're already too late. Maybe they're already here." I speak with a confidence I don't have. I know they aren't here yet, but I know they'll find me. And I know they'll rain down fire when they do.

"Keep dreaming, sweetheart. You are going to go up for auction and some wrinkly dick will buy you up and use you until you are just a broken thing that no one would recognize. Then he'll slit your throat and put you out with the rest of the trash. Now, you get one choice here. We can drug you to keep you calm and quiet, or I can put this chain around your neck so you don't get yourself into trouble. Up to you. The drugs cost money, but it sure would be nice to see you splayed here for the taking."

"You must be terrified of me if my choices are for you to drug me or chain me up in a locked room."

"Pick your poison, bitch."

"The chain." I grit past the pounding of my heart. He nods and the man behind me moves to get the chain from the wall. I want to struggle and fight back, but there's nowhere for me to run if I managed to take out two fairly large men with no weapon, and I don't want to get drugged. So I force myself to sit still while he hooks a heavy lock around my neck. It immediately starts to chafe my skin, and sits heavy and awkward, but I only glare at them.

"Sweet dreams. I'm off to post your pictures and see how many terrible people we can invite to your auction." He winks, and it reminds me of Enzo when he teases. I look away as the tears rise. I can't break while these men are still in this room with me. When they both leave, I scurry off the mattress and go to the corner of the room. The chain barely allows it, but I have just enough space to lean my head back against the corner and pull my knees up. I unstrap my heels and sit them beside me. I've used my shoes as a weapon before, I'll fucking do it again if I'm given the chance. Then I close my eyes and think of my men. They are coming for me. Whatever these men threaten, Aren and Enzo are coming for me.

27

AREN

I sit as the men around me talk. Ever since they told me they lost Lia's signal, I've been lost. They lost her. She'd been right there, they'd only been minutes behind, but men came in and took her, found her phone, and made Lia disappear. I've been in this world for far too long. I know all the things that they could be doing to her right now. I can't talk, I can't participate in this conversation because if I open my mouth, I'm going to throw up. My lead took me nowhere, except away from Lia when she needed me. I should have been there with her when those men broke in. She shouldn't have been left alone, but I trusted Enzo to keep her safe and trusted his word. If he didn't look just as broken as I'm feeling, I would rip his fucking head off. But I know when we get Lia back she'll want him too, so I let him live.

"I don't see anywhere obvious around where we lost the signal." Zane frowns at the map he has up on his computer. He sent some of the guns to search the area for the cars and anything suspicious, but he brought Enzo back to his house and Enzo had called me to tell me to meet them here. Zane wanted access to his computer, and he's been hunched over it with all kinds of crazy coding shit or something happening on the side of the screen while he squints at the map. He hacked his way into something very illegal to trace where they could be hiding, but I didn't have the capacity to listen when he was explaining it.

"I think I found something for you to trace." Romano speaks up from the corner of the room. He's staring at his own computer with a deep frown. All of us perk up and Enzo moves away from Zane to see what Romano is looking at. He's mostly been looking through our normal channels of information to see if anything pops up. I can hear Enzo swallow from where I am. His eyes dart up to mine and my heart falls straight through the floor. I come around and see the picture of Lia. Her face is bruised, her lip busted and swollen, and some man is holding her so tight I can see the indents in her skin where his fingers are. She glares at the camera, but there's fear in her gaze. They fucking hurt her and they made her afraid. They took her from me and I'm going to tear the world down for this. Whoever is near her when we find her will die a bloody death, that I can guarantee. Then I see the info at the bottom and curse aloud. Romano scrolls down and a few other photos of women pop up. Women they are planning to auction off.

"Send it to me." Zane orders tightly and Romano forwards the information so Zane can get to work. He only pauses when his phone rings. "Get that, will you?" He asks Enzo without looking away from his screen. Enzo holds it up to Zane's face to get it to unlock and answers with a curt "What?" barked towards the caller.

"Shit!" He yells only a minute later. "Fucking hell. Romano, I need you to take this." He hands the phone over and Romano stands, ready to get moving to whatever task Enzo just handed him. I watch Enzo run his hand through his hair and I see no sign of the usual flirty asshole he is. "They made a move and hit one of our restaurants. They played smart; got us distracted so they could take her. Now they have her and know that's where our focus is. This probably isn't the only hit about to go down."

"Get Mara." Zane says after only a pause, then his hands are flying over the keyboard again. "She can reach out and get everyone to shut down and get out. I don't want anyone getting killed and Lia is top priority right now. We get her back, then we deal with the rest of this shit."

I stare at Zane in surprise. I've liked him since we met and I've seen his devotion to my cousin and accepted their relationship easily. He's done nothing but make her happy and give her the world. But to see him put *the family* aside for *our family* gives me the absurd need to hug him. I resist. Instead, I offer to get Mara and leave the room while they work. Zane convinced Mara to take a break a few minutes ago when her anxiety started to get the best of her. Like me, she didn't have much to offer at the moment, and not having anything to do was making her pace. We all know he was just worried about her stress levels and wanted to keep her out of the middle of it, but when I find her staring at her phone, crouched on the ground with her dog Ani sitting on her, I know Zane didn't do anything to help her nerves. She's holding it together, but I can see the sharp edges of panic in her gaze.

"Any news?"

"Zane has something to trace now. But they are attacking businesses and he needs you to get everyone to close and get out. I can send word to the Papazian side of things, but can you handle Moretti? They've mostly been attacking those so that's the bigger danger, I think."

"Yes, finally. I need something to do." She stands and is already pulling something up on her phone. Ani stays pressed to her side as Mara walks towards me and folds herself into a hug. I'm not a soft man, but I've always been soft for her in a way I'm not for anyone else, even Lia. Mara is my blood and I've had to watch too much happen to her. I always knew she needed my love more than anything else. I couldn't really protect her, but I could be her family. I pull her into a bear hug until I feel her spine straighten. Someone answers and she's all business as she steps away from me and starts talking a mile a minute. I feel the loss of her comfort as she steps away and starts getting shit done. I'm not quite ready to go back, though. I make my own call to order our buildings to empty until we know what's happening. In the darkness, I only see Lia's face. I see what they did to her. I know Enzo watched as they took her. I know he heard it. That's a weight I don't want, but also feel like I need to see. I need to see every moment of this unfolding so I can make sure something like this never happens again.

Mara returns a few minutes later and nods. "All done. No one else has been hit yet, but that doesn't mean they won't be. We should go check on Zane. Maybe he has something."

I nod and tuck her under my arm. Ani follows, but Mara orders her to lie down before we enter the "war room". Zane's eyes go to Mara the moment she steps in the room. "It's done." She assures. "Do you have anything?"

"I have a lot of walls to get through, but I'm making some headway." He grunts, though his tone is softer. "We will get her back." He assures quietly. Enzo and I look at one another. Fuck yes, we will.

28

Enzo

"I've got them!" I jump from the boom of Zane's voice. It's been hours. Hours since Lia was taken and we've been sitting on our asses while she's been going through fuck all. I need her back. I need to see her and hold her, and kill everyone that's laid an eye on her since she's been gone. Dawn broke as Zane did his work, and the rest of us basically drifted in and out as much as we could.

Zane moves like he hasn't been up staring at a screen all night. Aren and I stand as one, following him as Zane sends a location to our people. Our order to go to war.

"I'm going with you." Mara is already on our heels and I watch as Zane's face goes white.

"Mara-"

"We are a team. We are in this together. I. Am. Going."

He nods tightly, but when he turns to look at us, we are given clear instructions to make sure she stays safe. He'll do everything he can to save our girl, and we are to do the same for his. Aren doesn't need the side-eye though; he's already taken up residence at her side as we go to the SUV. "Where are we going?" Aren asks as he takes the backseat with Mara. It will be easier to cover her there if needed and Aren is already planning for the worst. Zane gets in the driver's seat and takes off the second everyone is in.

"The auction is about to take place. We are going there."

"Fuck," Aren punches the back of my seat, which I know isn't personal, so I ignore it. I saw the video of her fighting off her kidnappers. I saw that she didn't let them move her one inch without a struggle. While I love that about her, I also fear that it will cause her more injury than what they might have planned. As much as I love her for being strong and not taking shit, I hope she knows we are coming for her. And I pray for everyone around her that they don't lay a hand on her. I remember going with Zane to get Mara from the locked basement at her father's. She'd gotten her revenge, but not without injury. The look on Zane's face when he saw her, and saw her blood, is something I will never forget.

"That was quick." I would think it would take longer to arrange an auction.

"Already on the books. They had other women already lined up, but they put her out there, saying that she was one of ours... We will get to her before anything happens. They aren't far."

I nod, but my mind is already reeling to everything that could have already happened to her, and all the terrible things those disgusting humans will have lined up for her. "Everyone is already called in?"

Zane nods and swerves through traffic, running through a light and edging a sidewalk to avoid a turning car. I feel like I'm done riding in cars with him for a while after all of this. I'm glad for his skills behind the wheel, especially when I don't think I have the ability to maneuver us right now while my mind is with Lia, but holy hell, we can't save her if we're dead. He pulls up in front of a warehouse building that's been refitted into a club. While the club itself is on the books, the things happening in the private rooms are surely a different story. Expensive cars surround the building, but the lot is otherwise empty. The party probably settled down with the rising of the sun. They must want privacy for their auction, which at least saves us the worry of killing an innocent when we go in guns blazing.

"Any idea how many women were in the auction? Our focus

is obviously Lia, but I'm not about to leave behind others if it can be helped. We get them all out and kill everyone with a dick."

Zane eyes me and I can see him thinking through the politics of it all. Anyone who is anyone could be in there to participate. We are going in without knowing all the players. But if saving some women from a life of torture means we are starting another war, then that's something I'm very willing to do. We've been working to end the skin trade as much as we can, but men with money don't like being told no. "We've made alliances. If we need to call them in, we will. We clear this building and get the women out. From what I saw, there were twelve listed."

"We can burn it down afterwards and do our best to make it look... accidental." Mara says almost cheerily from the backseat. She's frowning at the building, her hands fisted in her lap. She was almost married to a man in order to corner deals with this part of our world.

Cars pull up around us, the rest of our team. Romano is out first, gun already in hand as he takes the lead, getting the rest of the guns ready for their job. Then he approaches us and I roll my window down. We don't want Mara out in the open until we are ready, and we all need to be on the same page before we go in. "We clear the building. Get the women out, kill everyone else. Make it as clean as possible; we'll deal with all of it afterwards."

"We already have eyes on us," Romano states, nodding towards the building. There are cameras looking out towards the parking lot; none of us are surprised by that.

"They already knew we'd come." Zane says without worry, checking his own gun. "We don't know the guest list, but we aren't being choosy." He states, meaning we can take out badges, politicians, whoever dares to be inside the same building as Lia. "If anyone sees Vram, feel free to shoot on sight, but I want to know. His body needs to make a statement when all of this is done." His eyes flash to Mara's in the rearview. "Agreed?"

She gives one quick nod and reaches for a case under the seat. We watch her go through the motions of getting her own gun.

The order to keep her covered goes without saying. Everyone knows she's to be protected at all times. Any injury that comes to her, Zane will take out threefold on every guard that should have been watching her. We all get out and follow the lead, but Aren's hand comes down on my shoulder. He pulls me to a stop and stares me down.

"We get our girl back, and we show her what being ours means. Understood?"

"Sure, Daddy Dom."

"Fucking idiot." He groans, and we are on the move again.

The front of the building is a standard bar area. There are guns waiting for us, but our men move quickly. We don't worry about being quiet; everyone already knows we are here. We have enough men with us, we don't really need to put in our own effort just yet, so we keep a circle around Mara and monitor any side doors. The second room we enter is filled with a stage, stripper poles, and curtained off seating around the edges, clearly meant for private dances. There is glass on the upper floor, providing a view to admire the strippers. Aren and I point our guns towards those windows, looking for anyone with a gun trained on us.

We hit the center of the room and all the lights turn off. Everyone freezes. Then strobe lights start and an amused voice comes over the speakers. "You think I would make it that easy? I've had a year to watch how you work. A year to plan how I'll take control. This isn't usually the type of show I enjoy watching, but I do think I'll enjoy this." Then the gunfire starts, the flashes of guns mixing in with the strobe lights, the sound deafening as it fills the room. This was a trap.

29
Lia

I spent the night dozing in and out, jumping at every small sound. The building is busy. Even through the thick door, I heard muffled talking and movement throughout the night. I kept waiting for someone to burst into my room. When my door opens, my body is stiff, and my neck is chaffed from the chain. I hold my shoes as a shield as one man from yesterday stands at my door. He takes his time looking me over, so I give him the same look that would wither the balls of other men. Apparently I amuse him, because he chuckles and heads my way. "What are you doing?"

"Sleep well, princess?" He squats down just out of reach so I can't kick him.

"It's not my last day on earth, so I slept just fine. Can't say the same for you."

"Yeah, I know, you think they are coming to save you." He tilts his head, and the movement makes me think of Ani when she's trying to figure something out. He could be handsome if he wasn't evil. He has a goatee going, but it doesn't hide the little dimple that stands out when he smiles. He has a dark complexion and laughter lines around his eyes. Too bad he enjoys selling women or he might be able to find a willing one. "Too bad they are probably already dead. We left some breadcrumbs for them, but they didn't lead to you. Instead, they walked into a gunfight. I haven't heard the reports yet, but I know they went there, so," he shrugs, "you might want to get used to this new destiny of yours. Vram will take over, and you'll spend the rest of your days bringing pleasure to whoever pays the most for your pussy." He stands while my world falls apart. He doesn't know who was at the gunfight though, and he doesn't know who made it out alive. The people I love can still be alive and well, but if they aren't, it doesn't matter what's about to happen to me. I won't survive losing all of them, even if I get to spend the rest of my days in the comfort of my home, surrounded by luxury.

My thoughts spiral, but when he takes a step towards me, I chuck one of my shoes right at his head. It bounces off his forehead, but he just quirks an eyebrow at me. "You have a thing for shoes, don't you?"

"Come closer and I'll show you just how much I like my shoes." He bends over, but before I can hit him in the eye with the heel of my other shoe, he snatches it out of my hand and chucks it across the room. Then he drags me to my feet and pushes me against the wall, making my head bounce off with a painful thunk.

"I think you forget how much danger you're in. We are not to be trifled with. That's a first-class ticket to getting yourself killed."

I tilt my head. "But then how will you make any money off of me?"

Another man saves him from answering. He's new and covered in scars. One slashes across his neck and I can't take my eyes off it. I have no idea how he survived an injury like that. He comes close while my other buddy pins my arms at my side. The chain is removed from around my neck before he grabs one arm while the handsome one takes my other. "Where are we going?"

"To your auction. We have to get you cleaned up first, though." The two men drag me down a dingy hallway to a room filled with naked women and a wall with multiple shower heads and drains on the floor. A door shuts behind us and the men release me.

"Go ahead, strip."

I stare back at them, and acid turns my stomach. "Either you strip, or one of us takes your clothes off for you." The scarred man demands this time. I glance between them and take in the other men standing around the room. Women do their best to cover themselves, while others just stand staring off into space. The scarred man waves towards a small group of other men and they start towards us. They are huge and the thought of either of them touching me sends a jolt of fear that overruns my desire to keep my clothes. I lift my chin and do my best to disassociate from the moment. I remove my clothes as quickly as I can, not wanting it to be tempting like I'd originally planned when I dressed. I'd wanted my men to strip me slowly, finding the fun layers of teasing lace. I wanted their hands on me and their mouths- I cut that thought off as I remove the last pieces. I leave them on the tiled floor and am grateful the men only give me a cursory glance before waving me toward the showers. I follow the rest of the women and step under the spray of water that starts. I scrub my face, knowing it has to be smeared with makeup. The water is cold, and I don't know how long it will last, so I block out the eyes of the men in the room and scrub my skin. I'm not trying to get pretty for an auction, but I want the memory of all those hands erased from my body.

When the water shuts off, we're sent to another room where there are harsh looking women holding sheer white nightshirts. It's all we're given, so we pull them over our wet bodies. The shirt lands high on my thigh because of my height, but it's at least low enough to cover my ass. Though, with the sheerness of the material, and my wet skin, I know nothing about me is left to the imagination. My hands shake as my reality settles in. Until now, I've been in fight mode, just trying to survive until my rescue team showed up. But now I'm not sure if they are even alive. I have to push the thought away before I fall under a wave of emotions. Handcuffs go on each of us, and then we're ushered forward. Men take up guard posts on either side of us; a hand holds my elbow as an extra deterrent against trying to escape. Some women look drugged; they trip and shuffle their feet, following wherever the men are dragging. A few are crying while others just stare forward. Fear grips me like icy fingers pressing into my insides. I've seen Mara when she falls into a panic attack, and I wonder if this is how it feels. Those cold fingers squeeze until I'm not sure I have any air to breathe. We go out one door and I glimpse the sun before we are pushed into the back of a van. There's hardly room for all of us, but we press together while two men stay in the back before the doors close us into darkness.

The drive is quick, but it feels like it takes a lifetime. The panic wears off just enough for me to start thinking of an escape plan. I do not know what I'm about to walk into, but I think it might be easiest to let the auction take place and try to escape during whatever transfer takes place. There are too many men watching our every move right now, but the buyers are probably expecting a broken woman to be handed over. If I act like I have no more fight in me, then I might take someone by surprise and get away. I'll have to wait for a window to open and just take the moment when it comes. The doors to the van open from the outside, and we are shuffled into a building. This one has sultry lighting and dark velvet walls. We're pushed along until we reach an area that is clearly backstage. Our handcuffs are locked in place on a long chain along the wall.

None of the women dare talk. Sniffles still sound out here and there, but the fear that's settled in is the kind that freezes you in place. I strain to hear anything from beyond the large red curtain in front of us. I think of a play I was in when I was in middle school. I thought it would be exciting to be backstage and step through a curtain and become someone else. That's not quite how my middle school play turned out, but that feels like a pretty accurate description to my current predicament.

I can hear movement and deep chatter, but nothing is enough to give away any decent information. Not until someone's voice starts over the speakers.

"Welcome gentleman! We have some lovely choices for you this evening, and as advertised, we also have a special guest for our auction. Many of us have seen a decline in business since Mr. Papazian's death. Moretti taking over our streets has been most unwelcome, but tonight, we have something of his. One of his women joins us this evening, and let me tell you, she is a pleasure to the eyes. I'm sure whoever has deep enough pockets to take her home will get his money's worth. But we can't start with the main event! I promise, none of our women will disappoint this evening!" Clapping follows that promise and I wonder if I puke all over myself if anyone will still want to bid on me.

A large man comes back and removes one woman from our long chain. She is tiny, practically skin and bones. It looks like she might break under the man's gigantic hands gripping her arm. Her hair hangs past her shoulders, still wet from our shower. She keeps her eyes down on her bare feet as she goes past. I want to scream. I want to tell her to fight and run, but I bite back my words. There's no stopping the tears, though. They wet my cheeks, but I hold back any sobs so I can hear what happens next. The announcer, who I have a sneaking suspicion is the handsome man from earlier, goes over all her attributes before calling out numbers. I tune that out, not wanting to hear whatever price she goes for. Someone wins, and the woman is brought back to us. She's shaking so badly I can see it when she walks past. Then she's re-attached to the chain. Someone else comes back and attaches a string to her wrist with a number hanging off of it. Then the cycle repeats. Another woman is taken, her attributes listed, and amounts are called out. She returns and has a number attached to her.

After the fifth woman, a man comes for me. My fight comes back when his hand falls on my shoulder. I jerk out of his hold, shouting for him to keep his hands off of me. The man grabs me by the back of my neck instead, his fingers pressing in with warning. I remember my idea to seem broken so that I'm not watched as closely, so I go limp in his grasp and follow his lead through the curtain. The announcer smiles at me when I step onto the stage. His arms spread wide towards me. He is the handsome man from earlier. I really wish I'd been able to shove the heel of my shoe into his eye.

I'm pushed forward and nearly trip over my own feet.

"Here she is. Niece of Erik Papazian. Cousin to his daughter, Tamara. She's part of the inner circle of the Moretti family. They came onto our streets and took what was ours, so now one of you lucky bastards can own something of theirs. Just look at this beauty! That long blond hair, her firm ass," he grabs my arm and turns me, giving a very clear view of said ass for everyone in the audience. "Perky breasts and a pampered pussy. Just think of all the fun that could be had with a body like this. Add in her connections, and she is almost priceless. Almost." He starts the bidding for me, but when a paddle rises, a sharp bang fills the room. I nearly jump out of my skin at the sound. The man that just raised a paddle slumps over and crashes to the floor. It takes me a moment to figure out what's happening. Another bang shoots off, and another man sitting in the audience falls over, dead. Then the panic erupts as the big man takes hold of me and tries to shove me backstage. Then the gunshots go off at a rapid pace, multiple guns shooting and men falling dead before they even know where the shots are coming from.

They are alive, and they are here. Hope nearly chokes me as I try to fight the large hand from my arm. When the announcer steps towards me, I let the hand support me while I throw both of my feet at him, kicking him in the chest and knocking the wind out of him. He falls to his knees, but the man holding me drags me back, and I'm through the curtain before I can do anything else. But now I'm feral with the hope that they've come to get me. I kick and thrash against the hold. The other men are too distracted trying to loosen the chain from the wall so they can drag all the women away at once, but I don't let my guard get me to the chain. I don't stop until he finally loses his grip, and he drops me to the floor. My hands are still handcuffed, but I can run. I do without hesitation. The announcer apparently got his breath back before a bullet found his skull because he steps through the curtain right as I'm trying to run past, and something hits me hard in the face.

Pain erupts, and I fall in surprise. Someone grabs my hair and drags me back before kicking me hard in the ribs. I look up at the man and grin, even as I taste blood. "It doesn't matter. You're dead, and you know it." A moment later, his head explodes in a spray of gore that splatters all over me. He falls to the side, narrowly missing me, and then I see Zane standing there holding a gun.

"Hey, Lia. Fancy meeting you here. I was going to tell you a joke about time travel, but you didn't like it." He sends me a wink, and I take a minute to realize he's trying to tell a joke. I've learned he likes to do that sometimes, to Mara's exasperation.

He just shakes his head when I continue to sit on the floor, blood from the announcer slowly seeping into the white shirt. Zane holds out his hand and other sounds come back to me slowly. Gunfire is still going off like crazy, but a stillness is settling in around me. I turn and see the chain is on the ground and someone is slowly releasing the women one by one. Someone from our side then. Zane tucks me in under his arm protectively, mostly blocking me from view. I want to find words; I have questions I need to ask, but I just stare until every woman is freed from the chain. And then I cry.

30

Aren

It's a bloodbath, and I could swim in it all day if I didn't need to see Lia with my own eyes. I know Zane went to her since he had the easiest opening. We've been killing all day, and it's now settled into my bones like a habit that can't be crushed. We walked into a trap but we'd been smart about the use of our men, and though we lost a few, and a few others were injured, Zane had men crossing all paths of the building. It didn't take them long to hear the gunfire and get to the shooters. They hadn't banked on our numbers, and they'd leaned into their surprise and having the upper hand. But we walked away in the end. The men that weren't immediately shot sang like canaries after a few broken fingers.

"Go!" Enzo meets my eyes and nods towards where Zane disappeared. I know Lia is safe behind that curtain, but I need to see her. Enzo covers me, though there aren't many left to shoot at us, and I go down the steps so I can get to the stage. When I pull the heavy curtain aside, I nearly slip on blood coating the floor, but I right myself and spy the circle of women that are huddled together. Mara is coming to help them. We knew they might need to see a friendly female, but Zane refused to let her in until we had the building cleared. Not after she was shot at earlier. Mara agreed to wait outside until we freed the women, then she would can and help. She thought it would probably be better if she wasn't coated in blood when she came to them, which was the winning argument to keeping her away.

A slight panic hits me in the chest when I don't immediately see Lia with the others, but then I see Zane's back and realize he's holding someone. Lia. I run forward and my gut wrenches when I hear the sobs coming from her. I remember the day we found out about the accident that took our parents. Immediately I understood the danger that was coming for us with their death, and I questioned if it had truly been an accident or a grab for power that took them from us. But Lia had just been a grieving girl. She'd been a teenager who needed her mother to help her into womanhood. She'd been in a new place, in a new house, supposedly joining a new family. And then it was just me and her. She'd cried herself to sleep for days afterwards. That's when it really hit me that I needed to be her shield against the world. There was still an innocence to her that our family hadn't destroyed, and I didn't want the harshness of this world to take that away. But the sound of those broken sobs tells me I failed in my mission.

I come around Zane and find her covered in blood and shaking in his arms. He meets my gaze and gives me a small nod of reassurance. "Lia, baby..." I try to look her over, but Zane is still doing his best to hide her, not from me, but from the rest of the room. I see blood everywhere, but I know he'd be freaking out if it was all hers, so that helps me stay calm as I say her name again. This time, her head lifts, and my breath catches in my throat. She's covered in bruises and blood, some of which is definitely hers. "Aren!" She pulls back from Zane and throws her arms around me, burying her face in my neck. I lift her away from Zane and sit down on a bench against the wall, sitting her in my lap. The gunfire has stopped, so I know Enzo will join us any minute, but I tuck her against me for right now and run a hand up her back in soothing circles. Zane gives me a look before nodding towards the back of the building. He disappears that way and comes back a minute later with Mara. Mara glances towards us, but Zane leads her towards the other women, leaning forward to whisper something in her ear. I return my focus to Lia. I let her get her tears out and just continue to do my best to soothe her. It takes everything in me to hold myself together as she falls apart. I do not know the extent of what she's been through, or her injuries, but right now, I know she just needs me to hold her so she can safely crumble. Enzo appears and stares at us. He stops and looks her over slowly before glancing at me with a thousand questions. I don't have the answer to any of them; I only know that she's currently back in my arms and I don't plan on letting her out of my sight ever again.

Her tears fade slowly as the world continues to move around us. Then she lifts her head, and seeing the bruises marring her beautiful face is like a punch in the gut. "Hey there, baby." I brush a thumb gently over her swollen cheek. "Where are you hurt?"

She shakes her head and turns like she senses Enzo. Before she can hop out of my lap to run to him, he steps forward to gather her in his arms, sitting down next to me so she can still sit on me while he hugs her. "Hello, Sunshine. You missed date night." His hand tangles in her hair and massages her scalp. He kisses up her neck, avoiding the bruises on her face. I see the raw ring of skin around her neck, and rage threatens to strangle me.

"I want to get her out of here." I announce, gathering her back into my arms so I can hold her when I stand. Enzo steps aside to speak to Zane, and then he nods me over. I carry Lia like she weighs nothing, and for the first time in her life, she doesn't complain. She just holds me and tucks her face back into my neck. I know Mara wants to see her and talk to her, but she's focused on the other women and lets us go, knowing that we'll take care of Lia, but there's no one else to take care of the others. I know they'll get the women out and somewhere safe, and then they will decide the best way to handle this bloodbath. We don't know everyone in the building yet, but I'm sure there are people here that will give some blowback. They'll check for Vram's body since he wasn't in our little trap. If he's not here, then we'll go hunting. He won't live out the week if he's not already dead. And no matter how they decide to deal with this crime scene, it will be well known that we won't stand aside while our people are put in danger. Anyone that stands against us will no longer be tolerated.

They came into our home, and they took our woman. They put their hands on her and hurt her. I don't know if they did worse, but I'm not ready to ask that question, and I'm not sure she's ready to answer it. We reach one of our cars and Enzo takes up the driver's seat while I go in the back with Lia still curled around me. We leave in silence, Enzo looking at her through the rearview mirror every so often like he needs to check she's still there. She grows still and heavy in my arms and I realize she actually fell asleep in my lap, her head resting over my heart. "Can you have the doctor at your house? I want her checked over by someone we trust." I whisper over her head, but Enzo hears me and hits a few things on his phone. We pass the rest of the ride in silence as Enzo drives us home.

A car is already there when he pulls in. He gives me a nod to assure me it's the doctor and then comes around to open my door so I can climb out with her. She slept the entire ride and hardly stirs when I jostle her to stand. Enzo opens the door and waits for me to pass through before closing it behind us. I go to her room and lay her on the bed carefully.

Enzo walks in with the doctor a minute later. "What happened?" The man asks as he looks her over. The shirt she's wearing is sheer except for where it's soaked with blood. I want to shield her from his eyes, but I also know he's going to have to check every inch of her to make sure she's okay, so I force my hands into fists and step back so I'm near her head. "We don't know the extent of anything. They took her yesterday, and she fought back. After that, we can't say exactly what happened to her. We aren't sure what blood is even hers, but other than the injuries on her face, she doesn't seem to be actively bleeding." The doctor nods and then starts ordering us around. He wants her cleaned off so he can see her injuries better. He is careful as he listens to her heart and takes her blood pressure. Then he checks over every injury while we stand to the side. He has a nurse with him, and she works to clean Lia off. Enzo collapses into a chair he pulled up beside her bed, and I see the exhaustion hit him all at once. Now that Lia is back with us, he's letting himself feel his own needs. I'm not there yet, not until I know the extent of her injuries. Not until I know if Vram is dead. I pace until the doctor and nurse are done with their work. I watch their every movement and track every touch against her skin.

Once they're done, the nurse asks if there's something clean we'd like her in, so I get a set of comfortable pajamas and hand them over. I watch the nurse carefully dress her and tuck her under a new comforter after the bloody one is removed. "Is it okay that she's still sleeping?"

"Yes, I gave her some pain medication, which will help her sleep. She's probably exhausted after everything she's been through. Rest is the best medicine for her right now. There are no major injuries. She's got a lot of bruising. She was hit pretty hard in the face, the ribs, and the back of her head; but she'll heal. There are no signs of rape and no broken bones. I am worried about a concussion. I'll let her rest today and I'll come back to check on her tomorrow and ask some questions. If she has a severe headache, seems confused or has any issues with vision or hearing, call me immediately and I'll come right back. Otherwise, just let her rest. She can ice her bruises if they are bothering her and make sure she stays hydrated. Plenty of water, maybe have some soup for dinner. I'll come back in the morning." He waits until he's sure we've heard everything and then gives a kind nod before leaving us. We watch while Lia sleeps.

31
Enzo

We spend a week watching every move Lia makes. She was tired the first few days and mostly rested, but she's back to being herself and hating every moment we keep her in bed. Today she's just unreasonable.

"Enzo, I just want to take a long, hot shower by myself. Without the two of you hovering over me. I'm okay. I'm here. But as much as I appreciate you guys helping me bathe, I feel gross and I want an actual shower." She pouts from the bed. Her bruises look worse than they did when we brought her home. The coloring has changed as she's healing, but every time I look at her, I think of how I left her alone in my home and she was taken. Men I hired to protect her died, and our enemy got to her. "Enzo! Mara is coming over later to see me, and I want to shower!"

"Settle down, she-demon. I just think you should let me shower with you. I can help you reach those hard-to-reach places." I wink, but I'm already relenting. The doctor cleared her, and she might stab me with one of her shoes if I keep pushing her. Aren and I sat and ate dinner with her while she took us through everything that happened after she was taken from the house. She told us calmly, but I'd been anything but calm. I had to force myself to cheer her on when she told us how she fought back, and I held her gently when she was done. But when I left her room, I punched a hole in the wall. We watched the news together as a fire was put out in a local theater that puts on exclusive shows. Bodies are still being recovered and identified. Dark sites are quietly being released to news outlets showing exactly what kind of shows were put on in that theater. Links have now been made to human trafficking and each body that is identified is now being looked into. They don't know who is behind the deaths or the fire, but that seems to have fallen to the side as all this new information keeps coming to light. We know Zane has been doing his own research and sending the information out, keeping the focus on the human trafficking angle, and how each body was involved, and how they'd had previous involvement.

"Enzo," she smiles sweetly at me. "Until I've showered, you and Aren aren't getting anywhere near me. I feel gross and I know I look like crap. I need this."

I lean forward and press a soft kiss to her lips. She holds herself back, and that nearly makes me growl. "Don't say my girlfriend looks like crap. She looks beautiful and badass. You can take your shower by yourself, but you leave the bathroom door open just in case, deal?" She rolls her eyes, but I choose to ignore that when she finally relents. I sit on the bed and watch as she goes to the bathroom. She leaves the door open as I ordered, and the water turns on a moment later. I want to ask her if her head feels okay, but I bite the question back. I don't want her to have my blood on her hands, and I am about two questions away from her doing a murder.

Aren enters the bedroom with a tray of food in hand. He frowns at the space Lia should be in and then his head darts towards the bathroom. "She's fine. She needs some space. Did you bring me breakfast in bed, Daddy Dom?"

Aren ignores me. "Zane thinks he knows where the hideout is." He called in our alliances to warn them about the body count we left the other day, but he also wanted everyone to put ears to the ground to find this bastard. "He received a verified lead last night. He wants to move in and end the fucker."

I glance back towards the bathroom. No way in hell she's being left alone again, but it also doesn't feel right to leave Zane on his own to handle this. He may have an army at his back, but none of them are me. No one would have his back like I will and vice versa. I look at Aren. "I'll go with Zane. We can go while Mara is here and you can stay with them, along with some guards. Zane and I will make sure this is over, and you can make sure our woman is safe. We can't leave her without one of us again."

He surprises me when he doesn't argue. He knows it's just as important to make sure Lia and Mara are safe as it is for us to bring down Vram. Aren nods. "Make the call." He chucks something at my head and I barely dodge it in time. "She gets a whole tray of fruit and shit and I get a protein bar chucked at my head? What kind of relationship is this, anyway?"

"One where I tolerate your presence."

"In my own house?" I feign a gasp of surprise.

We both turn towards the bathroom when the shower shuts off. It takes a minute before Lia, wrapped in a towel, moves in front of the doorway. Aren and I both watch as she brushes her hair and adds some lotion type stuff to it. She brushes again and then pulls out the dryer. She's in full getting ready mode, so I call Zane to tell him I'm good to go with him today after he brings Mara here. We discuss how many guards to leave at my house and struggle to settle on a reasonable number knowing that my house has already been infiltrated once. Aren staying to watch over his cousin and our woman probably counts as ten men by himself. Zane and I get off the phone just as Lia finishes brushing her teeth and turns to find Aren and I watching her. At some point during her little show, Aren sat the tray of food down and took up a seat at the edge of bed.

She rolls her eyes but then grins. "Are the two of you getting in a morning snuggle? Don't let me interrupt. I just need some clothes-"

"No you don't." Aren states. She pauses to look at him. I can practically feel the heat coming off of his body as he stares at her. We've held her when she slept, and we've covered her in kisses, but neither of us has dared to touch her otherwise. Her arms and legs are still marred with scratches and bruises, and her poor face still looks painful to touch. I know it must still be painful because, despite her spending time getting ready this morning, she didn't put on a touch of make-up. She doesn't need it, but I also know that she enjoys wearing it, just like she enjoys getting dressed up and prancing around in her heels.

"I'm sorry, are you trying to be Daddy Dom right now? Because I only did a quick shave and I still look like," she waves her hand in front of her face like we can't see her injuries. "You don't want to play with me just yet. Come back in a week and we'll discuss-" She starts to walk around the bed towards the closet, the closet she tried to hide in when a group of men broke in and dragged her out of here.

"Stop." Aren's voice is more of a growl now. I want to warn him not to push her, but I don't miss the flare of heat that flushes her cheeks. She needs this so that she can feel like herself again. Aren sees it, and I know he'll make sure she's safe and taken care of, just as I will. Whatever he leads us into, because he *is* Daddy Dom, and he will be the one leading, I know Lia will enjoy every moment. "You may enter that closet, and you may bring out one thing to put on. A pair of heels. If you try to put anything else on, I'll spank your ass. Is that understood?"

"Do I get to keep my oh so fancy towel?" She sneers.

"Sure," he shrugs, "but not for long."

Lia gives him the middle finger, grabs a melon slice from the tray on the dresser and goes into the closet. She comes back a minute later looking two inches taller in strappy red heels. My dick instantly gets hard and my mouth goes dry. The towel is still knotted around her, but with her heels and the sway of her hips, she might as well be wearing couture. "Hot as fuck," I whisper, which earns me one of her sparkling smiles.

"Enzo is the one with the shoe kink; why don't you show him

what you chose? He might need to see you up close."

Fuck yes, I do. I sit up and turn my body so my legs are hanging off the bed. "Let me see, Sunshine."

32
Lia

Sunshine. I love the way Enzo calls me that. It makes me feel like I glow in his presence. I know they've been careful around me since I was abducted and almost sold to the highest bidder. Even though the discomfort of my bruises has faded, I know I look terrible, and it's been hard to have them following me around. I know they need to see that I'm alive, that I'm safe, but I just want to hide until I'm healed and then present myself how I want. I don't want them to see me while I'm like this, while I still feel a little broken.

Mara was upset that I kept pushing her visit aside, but while I can't avoid my men, I figured I could at least hide from Mara and Zane for a few days. I only got her to stay away by agreeing to her visiting me today, no matter what. She's been sending me updates about the other women that were with me. Other women that were saved because people came looking for me and refused to leave them behind. Women that probably would have slipped away into darkness if I hadn't also been taken. I know Mara has made it a mission to end human trafficking; I know she and Zane have worked to topple that particular castle, but I also saw firsthand just how many people are still falling through the cracks. There's still so much darkness in the world that we can't stop.

"Lia, he's waiting for you." Aren's demanding voice brings me back to the moment. To him sitting at the edge of my bed, his dark gaze observing me. Enzo is staring at me with open hunger on his face. He calls me sunshine, but he adds so much warmth and brightness into my life. And the man's one request was for me to come to him in heels and nothing else. Well, right now I'm still rocking this towel, but I think he'll probably enjoy taking it off of me. I only give the bruises on my ribs a single thought before it's replaced by images of him slipping his fingers or his tongue between my legs. Oh, yes. My body is all kinds of awake at that thought. I go to him slowly and stop just out of reach. I lift one of my legs to place my heeled foot beside him. The towel parts and I know he can see my most intimate places.

"Did I choose wisely? Or do you prefer another pair?" I ask coyly, twisting my ankle so he can see all the angles of my foot, even as I watch his eyes track up my leg to that part in the towel.

"I think he's having trouble appreciating your shoes because of that towel. Maybe you should lose it." Aren's voice is lower now, a velvety order that lets me give up control while I just enjoy what's happening in the moment.

"Okay, Daddy." I wink at Aren, but he just watches me with that steady gaze of his. Baring myself for the two of them while I still feel raw and exposed should feel hard. But they steady me, they love me, and they came for me when I wasn't safe. Trusting them with my body is as easy as breathing. One gentle pull undoes the knot of the towel, and it falls to the floor at my feet. Enzo's grin grows as he takes me in. "I don't know, Aren. He seems more distracted now."

Enzo makes a face. "Fuck yes, I'm distracted. You're gorgeous."

"Maybe you should come back to me then. Let him watch how your body looks in those heels as you walk away." Aren pats the spot beside him, but I see the pout Enzo makes, so I lean forward to give him a light kiss before I turn and give him the full view of my ass. I sway my hips in a gentle tease as I go to Aren. He frowns at me when I get to him, though. "I don't remember telling you to kiss him."

"I improvised. I'm also breathing, and you didn't tell me to do that either."

Enzo snorts, but Aren's eyes narrow. A ball of warmth fills my stomach at that look. "You've earned yourself a punishment with that mouth of yours. Come and take it like the brat you are." I want to talk back some more, but I also want whatever he has planned for me, so I take a step closer. "On the bed, on all fours, ass in the air."

I chew on my lip in hesitation before I climb up on the bed. I'm facing Enzo again, and the man is taking far too much enjoyment in this. He's watching with his pants tented in lust. "Should I take care of that for you?" I eye him, but he just shakes his head.

"Not until Daddy Dom tells you to. I don't want you in more trouble than you're already in."

Aren's palm comes down on my ass cheek with no warning. The sting spreads across my skin and I yelp to Enzo's amusement. Aren's large, calloused hand soothes away the burn before he does it again on my other cheek. "Aren!" I cry out, but he just chuckles darkly and repeats the soothing rub.

"Enzo, maybe you can get between her legs and help distract her." I don't understand the meaning until Enzo lays down and scoots under me, so we are in a 69 position. Then he's tugging me down so he can bury his tongue inside me. "Oh," I let out a soft moan just as Aren slaps my ass again and the sensations blend together until I'm a shaking mess as the two of them work me in their own ways. "Please," I finally beg as I hang right on the edge.

"Take out Enzo's dick and show him how much you love him, Lia. Suck him down your throat and I'll let you come." Aren punctuates his words with another slap against what must be reddening skin. Enzo's tongue slows. He uses his hands to support me as I undo his pants and pull his cock free. I fall on him, taking him deep and holding the rest of him with my hand, twisting and pumping as I support myself with my other hand. He keeps one hand on me to keep me balanced, but he goes back to devouring me, his free thumb coming up to rub at my clit. Aren slaps me again, close to where Enzo is eating me out, and the slap just sharpens everything Enzo is doing to me. Then Aren nudges a wet finger against my ass. He soothes me with his other hand when he feels me tighten, but he works slowly until his finger is inside me to the second knuckle.

"How do you like that, baby? You enjoy us worshiping you? You like being the center of our fucking universe?"

I answer with a moan against Enzo's cock, which has him moving faster against me and tilting his hips to get his cock deeper inside my mouth. "Hmm, I like this. Maybe we should keep one of our cocks in your mouth all the time. Stop that smart mouth from talking back." Aren retreats, only to return with two fingers. I gasp and nearly choke on dick. Aren just chuckles. "I finally get some peace and quiet when the two of you are eating each other out. Enzo, make her come."

I thought Enzo was giving me everything, but he flattens his tongue so he's stretching me and his thumb moves faster against my clit. Aren pushes his fingers deeper inside my ass and spanks me again with his free hand. I explode after hovering right on the edge for too long. I must drench Enzo's face, but he just takes me in and keeps working me until the hard pulsating of my pussy finally stops. I forget about his dick and simply collapse against him, but he doesn't seem to mind. Aren retreats first and disappears to the bathroom for a minute. He washes his hands and comes back with a warm towelette, which he uses against my tender flesh after moving me off of Enzo and laying me on the bed.

"Go ahead, Enzo; you can praise her." Aren grunts, but I glare at him.

"If I was good, then I want to hear you admit it, Aren. Go ahead, shower me in praise."

"And she ruins it the moment her mouth is free." Aren shakes his head at me. He stands and strips and I forget I'm supposed to be giving him a hard time. "You took your deserved punishment so well. And you are good at not arguing when your mouth is otherwise occupied."

"You are so bad at this." I shake my head and Enzo snorts his agreement before sitting up to press kisses against my collarbone.

"That's why I told Enzo to do it. But now you don't get his praise because you argued with me. Now you're stuck with me."

Enzo stops me from arguing further when he pulls my mouth to his. I can taste my release on his lips, but that somehow just makes the kiss more sensual. Enzo takes his time with me until the rest of the world melts away. I would even forget that Aren was watching if it wasn't for the heaviness in his gaze. I can practically feel his hunger as he watches what Enzo and I share. Then Enzo is stripping his clothes away, only moving his mouth away from me long enough to pull his shirt from over his head. Then he's pulling me on top of him and his dick is inside me with no warning. "Enzo!" I hold on to him as he grinds so that he's so deep he's touching places I'm not sure have ever been reached before. I feel him everywhere; my already sensitive skin takes everything he gives me and amplifies it.

"You can take so much more than that, Lia. You want us both? You want two men to love you and worship you? Then you better be ready to take us both. You better be ready to calm the hunger in both of us. Are you able to do that, Lia? Can you handle two men?" Aren's hands come to my hips and he moves me up and down, bouncing me on Enzo's cock. "Are you really the good girl that Enzo thinks you are?"

"She can take us both. In fact, I think she'll run us ragged." Enzo grins at me like his cock isn't doing things to my insides. My hands go to his chest, and I can feel his heart pounding under my palm. Aren opens something and then I feel a cool liquid against my ass. His thumb follows, rubbing in the liquid. *Oh.*

"Are you just going to talk about it, or are you going to put me to the test, Aren? Maybe you're afraid you can't handle me?"

"That's my girl," Enzo chuckles again before lifting his head to nip at my breast. Aren doesn't answer. A moment later, his cock answers for him. I feel him against my ass, spreading that liquid more and more with this thick cock. And then he's pressing against me. Not quite entering, but pushing against me before retreating, and then repeating. Each time, he presses a bit deeper, until he actually pushes his tip inside me. All of us still until Enzo moves so he can rub a finger against my clit. Then he pushes deeper while Aren retreats. Then they switch, Enzo going only to the tip while Aren pushes deeper in my ass.

"God, oh," I'm not sure I'm even forming words. I'm made of nerve endings that are firing off like crazy.

"You okay, baby?" Aren's voice is softer now, checking in with me. Instead of answering with my words, I press back against him, taking him deeper. Then I lean forward to pull Enzo into another deep kiss. And I'm surrounded and filled with the men that love me.

33

Enzo

Lia goes soft in my arms as our mouths tangle. The brattiness leaves her and she's just there in the moment with us. She's so warm and tight against my cock I almost fear I'll end too early. I don't want this to end. I want us all connected like this for the rest of my damn life. For the first time, I realize what a great position I'm in. I am seeing everyone in their most vulnerable moment. I can see Lia's thick lashes laying against her cheeks as she's filled with the both of us. I can see her mind turn off as she gives herself over to the sensation of it all. I can feel the pulse deep inside her as she orgasms. She shakes against me and I track the small tear that slips down her cheek as it all becomes too much for her. But I also see Aren as he gives himself over to the moment. He's usually so guarded, but right now, he's living and breathing Lia. That's all he feels and all he hears and his face is set in wonder at that. He holds her hips tightly as he uses her and gives her everything he has to give. Only I am able to see both of them in this moment of content weakness. As much as I want to be deep inside her ass, I realize this is a gift. We are a family now. Maybe not the most conventional, but we'd live and die for one another, and our universe is centered on this woman shaking between us.

I take in her beauty as I feel my release settle at the base of my spine. I want her to open her eyes and see me as I come deep inside her. I brush my fingers against her flushed cheeks and her eyes open as though she heard my silent request. She stares down at me and gives a soft smile. "I love you." She whispers the words, her voice raw after screaming with her release. Those three words undo me. I reach up to dig my fingers into her hair as I slam deep and coat her insides with my seed. I feel the slide of Aren's dick as he fully buries himself and gives her his own release. We both fill her up and I know the moment we pull free she'll be dripping with us. Lia shakes again with aftershocks and the pulse of her sends both Aren and I groaning. Then, Lia falls forward, laying against my chest, her sweat mixing with mine as we both struggle to catch our breath. Aren slides free first and Lia makes a small, pitiful sound at his loss. He stops and leans forward to cover her shoulder in tender kisses. "You were wonderful, Lia. You took us so well. I love you." His tenderness causes Lia's muscles to tighten and I give another small groan as my sensitive cock feels her inner muscles pulse.

"I love you, too. I love you both." She sighs tiredly, snuggling against me as Aren disappears into the bathroom. I reach for one of her hair ties on the side table and pull her hair back so I can tie it in a messy bun on top of her head. It doesn't look great, but it's just to get her through the hot shower I hear Aren start. She lifts her head to grin at me. "Did you just pull my hair back for me?"

"You already fixed it. But, not regrettably, we did just get you very dirty again. So you might want to get that fine ass back in the shower."

"I can't move."

"Sure you can."

Lia seems to think about it for a minute and then shakes her head. "Nope. Sorry, I am made of jello, and I'm going to make a mess when I stand up."

That makes me grin. "Fuck yes, you will. We filled you up, didn't we?" She answers with a groan, but only protests a little when I sit up with her and scoot to the edge of the bed. Then I move her legs so she's forced to stand, and I pull my cock free. I watch as my come spills free and then turn her so I can see the mess Aren left. "Fucking hell. Seeing you covered in us is way hotter than it has any right to be." I drop to the floor and kiss her knees before I slowly remove those heels she teased me so well with. Lia doesn't fight me, just rests her hands on my shoulders to support herself as I lift each foot in turn, our come making tracks down her legs the longer I leave her standing. "I suggest you hurry off to that shower before I pin you back down on this bed and fill you up some more." I take in her reddened skin from Aren's hand and reach out to squeeze gently, feeling the warmth of her skin against my palm. I am one lucky bastard. She turns to glare at me and then steps away before running off to the bathroom as I'm sure more of our come starts a faster descent down her legs. I'd laugh if I wasn't truly turned on again. Maybe Aren was right when he asked if she was going to be able to handle the both of us. If she has the same effect on his cock as she does mine, then her poor pussy is looking at a life of being used shamelessly.

"Are you joining us?" Her voice calls from inside the shower.

We take far longer in the shower than we should, but Aren and I both keep getting distracted by all Lia's body has to offer. The bun I so kindly did to her hair is lost as we forget ourselves and move her under the spray. Aren kindly goes to his knees and washes every inch of her while I keep her standing. By the time we both make her come again, and then finally get cleaned off, the water is going cold despite my very large water heater. I earn my name as a bad man based solely on my water usage in a state that is very often in a drought. Aren and I leave her to get ready while we go to our separate rooms to get dressed. The moment I'm ready, I'm back in Lia's room ordering her to eat some of her food after I belatedly realize we never gave her the chance to have her breakfast.

"I'm a grown woman, Enzo. I can take care of my own eating, thank you." But she takes the ice water I hand her and drinks more than half of it.

"We just thoroughly used your body, Lia. Drink your water

and eat your food. Rest and eat until Mara gets here so you don't pass out and then have to awkwardly explain that we sexed you unconscious."

"Sexed me unconscious?" She scoffs as she brushes some mascara across her lashes. Apparently now she's ready to face some make-up application. She doesn't do her whole face, just some mascara and some gloss on her lips, and I'm not sure if she feels like she needs it like a mask for company, or if we just made her feel more like herself that she wants to put on something she normally would.

"Keep arguing with me and I'll get the bossy one. Remember, you're supposed to be bratty for Aren and a good girl for me. That's the deal."

"I don't remember agreeing to that. I think I enjoy being bratty all the time. I want to see how long it takes for mankind to collapse under my heel."

I eye the heels that are sitting next to the bed. "Trust me, if anyone saw all the things you can accomplish in heels, mankind would have already fallen. You're a fucking menace to anyone that likes vaginas."

She snorts, and the unladylike sound makes me love her all the more. "So, you missed the conversation, but Zane thinks he knows where Vram is hiding out. I'm going to give him some back-up while Aren stays here with you and Mara."

"What?" Her brush clatters against the sink as she drops it in surprise.

"We are taking a ton of men with us, but I don't like the idea of Zane going without me. I have his back, and he has mine. That's the way it's always been. But we are also leaving a small army of men here with Aren. Nothing is going to happen to you again, Lia, I swear it. I don't care how many guards we leave with you; one of us will always be with you. I'm never trusting anyone with your safety again."

"I'm not worried about me." She waves that away like I'm an idiot for thinking of her safety. Like she wasn't just abducted from my house with guards left behind to watch over her. "Do you know what you're walking into? How many men does he have? He could set another trap-"

"We'll be safe. If you think Zane would do anything that would take him away from Mara, then you're crazy."

She frowns. "What about you doing something that would get you taken away from me?" I lean against the counter, crowding her against it until her eyes go wide. "What do you think, Sunshine? Would I do something that would leave you behind? I've seen how terrible Aren is at praising you, and my sunshine needs some praise. I can't leave that up to him." I kiss her bruised cheek gently, my only way to show her I know she's strong, I know she's not breakable. I saw her get taken, I saw her fight back, and I see her standing on her own two feet now. I still remember finding her in the hotel room covered in blood after saving her own life. But despite all that strength, she has a huge heart. One that is large enough to love both me and Aren. And a heart like that could shatter into a thousand pieces if she was hurt badly enough. I don't take that lightly. "I'll come home to you. You are stuck with me for many years to come. I don't promise that easily. I don't accept your love easily." I tuck her hair back and brush a finger across her chin. "I know what you've given me, and I treasure it. I treasure you."

Her lip quivers, but then she swallows back the emotions and gives me a curt nod. "Good. You should. I'm a fucking delight."

I smile despite myself and then pull her forward. I turn her so she's facing the mirror again. "Hydrate, eat, rest. Those are your orders until Mara gets here. Then you ladies can stay up and gossip and drink your man troubles away with a good girly movie."

"That was a little too on the nose." She squints at me like she's about to ask how many girl's nights I've been a part of. I slap her ass instead, and take a strange enjoyment out of the small squeal she makes. Then I leave her, hoping she'll do as she's ordered, but knowing she'll have to be left alone before she actually does it. Otherwise, she'd starve out of spite.

34
Aren

Zane and Enzo's plans for Vram go to hell not five minutes after Zane and Mara arrive. We are still discussing logistics when California shows its displeasure with humanity and shakes the earth hard enough to set off power lines. One minute, we were all talking and the next, we could feel the earth move from under our feet. It didn't last long, and it wasn't the strongest I've lived through, but the power in the area went down. Enzo had a generator that kicked on, but it changed our plans for the evening. Not knowing if other damage was done near where Zane and Enzo would need to go, and not being sure enough of the generator to risk leaving the house, they decided to leave their hunt for another evening. Once the excitement of the earthquake was over, Mara and Lia ran off to the living room to sit together and catch up after we've been "hiding Lia away" since we got her back. Mara isn't wrong, but as much as I love my cousin, I'm not sure how she expected anything different from us.

I watch them as they laugh and smile, each holding a glass of wine and sitting with their legs curled under them as they face each other on the sofa. The joy I see in Mara softens a shield I've had up since my father died. She went through so many years of pain and fear and now she's happy on the other side. Despite everything her father did, Mara came away from it all with a strength no one would have expected from her. Then I look at Lia, and I see all the years I stood as her guard. She stood at my side and helped me keep control of our house even as my uncle tried, *frequently*, to take it from me. Now he's gone, and I know she doesn't need me as a shield any longer. It's strange to feel peace while I look at the two of them. I don't think it's a feeling I'll ever get used to, and that's probably good. I don't want to get too at ease and miss danger. Our lives are still not normal, after all.

Zane comes to stand beside me and watches the women in silence for a minute. "Two guys walked into a bar, the third one ducked."

I look at him. I swear I'm surrounded by idiots. "Is there something special that was put in the water for Moretti men? I'm just wondering if it's something contagious or?"

"Don't know what you're talking about." He puts his hands on his hips and then shakes his head. "Fuck, my wife is hot." Then he turns to go back to where Enzo is sitting. He never called in some of the planned guns for the evening, but the ones he'd planned on leaving behind to watch over the house are patrolling outside. Despite the peace I feel while watching the women smile and relax, I feel like a caged animal. I don't know if it was the earthquake or the change in plans, but I feel unsettled. Ani comes to my side and rubs against my leg to stop my pacing, so I sit in a chair and give the dog some good scratches. Mara eyes us, making me wonder if the dog senses my unease. Ani stays at my side, so I keep petting her and try to place what feels off.

We all jump when a loud bang goes off outside. Then the generator cuts out, throwing us into darkness. Enzo had some candles going as a backup in case it flickered off, but it's hardly enough light. "Go," I order Ani back to Mara and I'm on my feet, all that earlier unease rushing through me now. My gun is in hand, the safety off and I'm going to the front door before anyone can say anything. Sure, it's probably just the generator going, but over the years I've learned to trust my gut, and my gut is screaming danger. I open the door just as gunshots fill the air.

"Fuck! Protect Lia and Mara!" I yell back to Zane and Enzo before I enter the fray, slamming the door shut behind me. I use the darkness to my advantage and duck down, trying to place where the danger is coming from. Our guards were spread around the house, and I wish I had my phone on me to shout an order for them to stay in place. I don't want them all congregating in the same place, leaving openings for the enemy to get inside. One of our men passes by me, only to fall dead a moment later as a bullet sails through his skull. Blood sprays in the darkness, but the shooter gives away their position. I shoot and hear him fall, but I don't know if he's dead, so I move quickly, finding cover. My body moves on instinct, my heart beats a regular pulse, and any of that earlier uneasiness is gone as I fall into a moment of life and death. I know everyone I care about is on the other side of these walls. I hear the gates moving and know more are coming. They got the generator down and now they can get in. I go to another spot, where I'm hidden from the driveway but will have the upper-hand against anyone that drives in. An SUV pulls in with their lights off and stops before letting out a small group of men with guns. The moment I shoot I'll give myself away, but I need to take out as many of these men as I can to protect everyone inside. I shoot the two on the driver's side before they can shoot back. More of our guns round the house and shoot the men on the other side of the SUV. I breathe out a sigh of relief, feeling more in control now.

I make sure the men see me and know who I am before I approach so I don't get a taste of some friendly fire. "They came through the gate. We need to keep others from getting in. Can you secure it until we can figure out the power?" The two men agree and run off in that direction. Bodies are scattered around the front yard. As far as I can tell, the danger is gone, but we have a major cleanup on our hands. Enzo's home is secluded enough that we might get away with the gunfight, but that's a big enough question to make me worry. Either way, I know it's time to head back inside to reassure everyone and have Zane check in with the rest of his men to make sure we are secure once more. My hand lands on the door when I hear movement. My hand goes to my gun, but a small tutting sound and the feel of cold metal against my temple has me freezing in place.

35

Lia

The darkness makes me feel ill. The erratic gunfire outside sends my mind racing to all the terrible things that could happen. Men that work for us are out there, men who trust Zane and Mara enough to put their lives on the line. I don't want to lose any of them, but I'd be lying if I said I was only thinking of them. My heart is solely worried over the safety of Aren. Zane and Enzo move Mara, Ani and I to the dining room, which is more centered in the house and has no windows. They are talking to one another about plans, about the patrol that's happening outside, but I only hear the words without real comprehension. Mara and I carry candles with us and Enzo grabs us flashlights from the kitchen on our way. He and Zane each take one and carry them crossed with their guns so they can see where they are aiming. Mara reaches out and holds my hand while Ani presses against us. We don't talk; we need to hear everything happening, and we need to know if anyone is inside the house. Zane and Enzo are acting as the last defense in case the patrol and Aren don't stop men from getting inside.

My mind spirals to the day I hid in the closet and was dragged out by my hair. I've been tired enough that the memories haven't haunted me in my sleep, but that doesn't stop all of that fear from nearly choking me now. There is a long quiet as the gunfire outside stops. Zane had an extra gun on him and gave it to Mara, but I'm without a weapon. I know how to shoot, but I never needed to carry a gun around with me. Aren was always at my side with a weapon within reach. Now I eye the gun in Mara's hand and feel useless without one. The front door opens, and we all tense. Zane steps closer to the doorway, and Enzo steps in front of Mara and I.

"I suggest you drop your weapon in case I get a little trigger-happy."

Zane moves slowly to place his gun on the floor. I can't see what's happening, but I recognize that voice. Enzo turns towards us and nods to the other doorway out of the dining room. We can't see what's around the corner yet, but Zane lowering his gun tells enough of the story. And I know Vram has finally made another appearance. I'd never forget the voice of the man that let me know my destiny was to be sold off to the highest bidder. Mara and I move quickly and as quietly as we can to leave the dining room. If we can get out of view, then we might find another way to fight back before anyone gets hurt. Ani takes off running. The tap of her claws against the floor feels like it echoes through the entire house, but we make it out and Mara opens the door to the pantry and pushes Ani in. Then she grabs my hand and we run down the hall. We can circle back around so that we come back to the dining room from the same side as the intruder, and because we'll be coming from deeper inside the house, we'll see them before they see us.

"Are you able to pull up the cameras? Did Enzo give you the code?" Mara whispers as we stand in a corner so no one can sneak up behind us.

"Enzo won't even tell me where the damn camera in my room is."

Mara rolls her eyes in understanding. "Men. Okay, do you know of any guns hidden? It'd be better if we both had one."

I nod, knowing that Aren has a few in his room. We have to cross the hallway, which will be in view of the main door if anyone is still out there. The darkness of the house will help keep us covered, but it also helps any intruder from staying out of view. Mara peeks her head around first and, when she sees it's clear, she nods for me to run. I trust her to cover me as I dart across the hallway and run up to Aren's room. I find one of his guns sitting ready on his dresser and do a quick check to make sure it's loaded before I remove the safety. Mara and I make eye contact from across the hall and then we nod and head back towards the dining room. There doesn't seem to be anyone else in the house, but we can hear talking as we get closer. Both of us slow so we can try to assess what we are walking into.

"I wonder if the women will come out of hiding if I blow his brains out?"

"I already told you they aren't here. It's girls' night, they went out to eat." Zane answers tightly.

"I think it's time for you to face the truth; there are three of us and only one of you. All of your men are gone, and it will only be a matter of time before our guards outside come in to check on us." Enzo sounds calm, and his calmness soothes the racing of my heart enough for me to gain some semblance of control.

"You overplayed your hand, Vram. You made a good run at seizing control, but if you shoot him, you'll be the next to fall. There's no way for you to win. But we can turn a blind eye while you slink back off into hiding. You can try your hand at an honest life. Find a nice woman to fuck until you die of old age. Or you die here tonight."

He has Aren. All of it makes sense now. Zane saw Vram holding Aren with a gun to his head. That's why he lowered his weapon. Mara reaches out a hand to grab my arm, but I'm no longer in charge of my body. I ready my gun and walk slowly into view of the doorway. I take in all the details of the candle-lit room before me. Aren and Vram have their backs to me. Vram is shorter than Aren, but the gun at Aren's temple is enough to keep him from fighting back. At least until he knows where Mara and I are. Zane is standing just in front of Enzo, clearly doing what he can to protect his friend and keep some shield between him and the man with the gun. Enzo sees me first, but his eyes move right over me like I'm not there. The only sign I have that he actually noticed me is the line of tension his lips become. I have the upper hand. I can aim and shoot without Vram even knowing I'm here. But Aren is right there, and I'm not sure if I trust myself not to miss. I'm also not completely confident he won't shoot Aren just out of reflex.

"I'm willing to die if I take you with me, but I'd rather make sure I clean house. Maybe I'll just wait until those girls of yours are home. I got a good look at blondie. I would have made quite the payday with her. If I'd known you were going to get to her, I would have had my fun while I had the chance."

"Yeah, sorry about shooting everyone." Enzo answers drolly, raising one shoulder and then eyes Aren. "How about you just let him go? We put our guns down. We can sit together and have a little chat until the ladies of the house return. You can keep your gun, but we can at least sit and be comfortable. Who knows how long they will take once they have some wine in front of them?" Enzo turns his back on Vram, pulls out one of the dining chairs, and sits at the table, leaning back with the nonchalance of a man completely at home and safe. Zane slowly takes me in, takes in Vram with Aren, and then looks at Enzo, who is now propping his feet up on the table. Enzo gives him the smallest nod and Zane moves to the table to take up a seat across from him. Mara places the flat of her hand against my back, like she's silently telling me to just wait and breathe. I aim and wait for Vram to make his move. Anything can go wrong right now. One of the guards could come in to check on us, Ani could bark, Vram could misread a muscle twitch and I could lose Aren. But I wait. And I breathe.

"Fine," Vram lets go of Aren but keeps his gun in hand. "But I want you to call off all the guards and send them home. I'm going to call in more of my men and we are going to wait until your women are home."

"Okay, I just have to get my phone from my pocket. I'll put it on speaker so you can hear the conversation though, okay?" Zane keeps his hands on the table until Vram nods. He moves his gun from

Aren to Zane. Aren moves slowly to the table to sit next to Enzo. Mara moves silently beside me and aims her own gun. She gives me a nod and while Vram is watching Zane reach into his pocket, we both shoot. I aim for his back while Mara, a more practiced shot, goes for the head. The room explodes in noise as both of our bullets find their home and Vram falls dead to the floor.

36

Enzo

The moment Vram's body falls, Lia is on him. She walks right up to him and kicks him in the ribs, and then she keeps kicking. I'm on my feet and rushing towards her before the other men can react. I know she hasn't dealt with being taken. After sobbing in the theater, she's been calm and collected any time the subject has come out. But I'm seeing that pain rear its ugly head once more as she slams her foot into the lifeless body. At least I know he's truly dead and didn't magically survive those two gunshots like some horror movie villain. I want to let Lia keep working out her issues, but I don't want her to hurt herself, so I pull her into a bone-crushing hug. She's soft and warm, and she hugs me back just as hard. I lift her off her feet as she buries her face in my shoulder. I only realize she's still holding a gun when Aren gently takes it from her hand and lays it on the table behind us. Then he comes around and hugs her from behind, not pulling her from my arms, but joining in.

"Look at us, our first group hug. I feel like a group hug should have come before all the group-"

"Shut up, Enzo." Mara jumps in before I can finish my sentence. I release Lia just enough to reach out and pull Mara into our little huddle.

"That's my wife." Zane sounds exasperated.

"So? A little hugging between friends never hurt anyone." I let go of Lia with my other hand, letting Aren hold her against me so I can motion Zane over to join us. "Come on, big guy. I know you're feeling lonely. For every second you hesitate, my hand will inch closer to her ass-"

"The fuck it will." Aren cuts in before Zane has the chance to yell at me. "If you even think about another woman ever again, I'll have a knife specially made for Lia to gut you."

"Tough crowd." I grumble, but Zane joins in the group hug, so we stand there huddled together for a minute while our enemy bleeds out behind us.

Aren kisses Lia's cheek before he pulls back and breaks up the moment we were having. "Well, I'm highly pissed off that I ended up with a gun to my head tonight."

"I'm highly pissed off that I'm going to have to buy a new house. Having my home compromised twice is clearly a sign." Lia puts her hand in mine and then takes Aren's hand in her other.

"Guess you'll have to come set up your room at our other house while we find something new here."

Zane walks around the body with a deep sigh and then pulls out his phone. "Gotta say, Enzo, I miss the days when you were in charge. Too much damn cleanup on this end of things."

"You're in charge; you can literally make anyone do whatever you don't want to handle." I argue back.

"Oh, good." He hands me his phone. "Deal with this shit. I'm going to check with the men we have left outside and see if we can get this generator back up. Mara, why don't you show Ani you're okay before the poor girl stress-sheds enough fur for a whole other dog?" He kisses her forehead and then leaves to handle things outside.

"I liked our plan of going to Vram and leaving the mess on his turf better." I grumble, but I make the call to Romano. He's going to "lose" his phone at the rate we're calling him. I sit back at the dining room table while I explain the situation. He can be the one to reach out to the cleaners and send them my way.

"Generator is done for." Zane announces, always one to bring me good news. "We can all go back to my place for the night. Get some rest, let the cleaners handle this." He waves a hand at the body on my hardwood floors.

Everyone agrees, so we go our separate ways to pack supplies for the night. Then, Aren and Lia climb into my car. They are kind enough not to have sex on the drive over, which I appreciate. I don't think I can handle blue-balling it after the night I've had. When we get to Zane's, Mara and Lia go to the courtyard with Ani to let the dog run out some of her energy after the stressful night. Zane follows up with our men to make sure everything is being taken care of. We've had a lot of blood on our hands recently, so we also need to check in with all the allies we just worked so hard for. Don't want them getting cold feet, but it's also a show of our power and that we won't sit aside while people try to make fools of us. People came for us, they came for our name and our businesses; they came for our women. And they died. We coated the streets in blood and ruined the names of those involved.

When Lia comes inside, she heads right to me and crawls into my lap, lays her head on my shoulder, and lets out a tired sigh. Aren watches from his chair, but there's no jealousy; he actually looks content watching us snuggle. "Let's go to bed. I'm exhausted." I hug her tighter and then wait for her to stand.

"I'm the one that had a gun to my head." Aren grumbles.

"You had nothing to worry about. These ladies were hot as fuck saving your life."

"Watch it," Zane warns when I include his wife in my assessment.

"I cannot tell a lie. And watching these women kill will never get old." I hold up my favorite finger for Zane, and then touch the small of Lia's back to lead her from the room.

"He has a point." Aren pulls her to his side. "It was hot as fuck watching you shoot a man to save my life."

"There is something seriously wrong with you guys."

"But we're yours." I blow a kiss in her direction and her

cheeks turn a pretty shade of pink even as she rolls her eyes at me. We all strip silently when we reach the bedroom I always use when I'm here. Aren and I take turns covering her in kisses but we don't take it farther than that, just go under the covers and lay skin to skin, Lia warm and soft between Aren and I. She turns towards Aren and pokes him in the chest.

"No more guns to the head, okay?"

"Sure, baby." He leaves soft kisses across her cheeks and the tip of her nose.

"So compliant." She sighs happily, snuggling into his chest while I wrap my arm around her to pull her ass against me. She curls her legs so they bend around mine.

"For tonight. You've earned my compliance after shooting a man for me. Now go to sleep, baby. We've got you."

"Love you both." She whispers as her eyes close.

One Year Later

Aren

Lia brushes her long hair over one shoulder. She added bouncy curls to it tonight and did some long line with her eyeliner on her top lid. Her lipstick is red, matching the bottom of her heels, and the black dress she has on holds tight to all of her curves. She's fucking devastating. And the little minx knows it. The grin she flashes me tells me all I need to know.

"No way in hell Enzo makes it through tonight with you looking like that." I cross my arms over my chest and lean against the doorway.

"I certainly hope not."

"Come on, trouble." I hold out my arm and she tucks her hand there. She smells like jasmine, and I want to bury my nose against her skin to see if she smells like that all over. The limo is waiting for us in front of the house we looked for together. It's a bit farther from society, but it comes with a lot of land and makes for a nice retreat when we don't have to be at the center of the Papazian and Moretti world. Lia hired gardeners and created a whole oasis outside that all of us have enjoyed, sometimes without our clothes on. We spend a lot of our time in our old home to monitor things and attend meetings, but when we know we won't be needed for a bit, we come up here and enjoy the peace. Sometimes we have Zane and Mara over, but more often than not, it's our little escape.

She and I climb into the back of the limo, and I'm a gentleman and keep my hands to myself. I know Enzo and I will get to have our fun after the speech he has to give. Thanks to the alliances we've made, our hold on our territory has strengthened and spread. One of our own was put in place for our state senate and Enzo is giving a speech at a dinner tonight to congratulate him. After the work that was done to dig up all the information and bring down anyone connected to the human trafficking incident that happened last year, our man was praised for all of his hard work. Zane did most of that work, but he got to select the man holding the power in public, so he got his own reward.

Lia and I walk together, my body a natural shield against her and the world, just as it has been since we were teenagers. Some things never really change. Zane and Mara are already at the table reserved for us, and Mara rises to hug each of us the moment she spots us.

"They have any food at this thing?" I ask after I push in Lia's chair and take up the seat next to Mara so there is still an empty chair on Lia's other side. Mara is practically glowing tonight, and Zane takes her hand in his the moment she's sitting next to him again. We've had a busy year, but it's been one of relative peace. We gained control of most of the weapons coming in and out of our state. We continued to uncover lines of human trafficking, and we've made all our findings public, giving us more power as we show everything that's being stopped. Using our alliances, we've helped others follow our lead. There is still plenty of danger and darkness in our world; that's something we'll never be without, but we've been able to control the worst of it. Now that we are getting a footing in politics, we can spread our power.

"Of course not. You pay thousands of dollars for a table, and they give you some fancy drops of food like it's nourishment." Zane responds with annoyance.

"Well, that money we pay goes towards a charity." Mara nudges him. "Besides, you know you ate a full meal before we left. So don't act like you'll starve."

"You're supposed to be on my side." Zane brings her hand to his mouth and nips at one of her fingers.

"I'm on the side of the truth."

A woman comes to the stage and quiets the room to announce Enzo. He's been gone most of the day to get ready for the event. His eyes scan the room as he introduces himself, and his stance changes when he finds our table. He gives the rest of the speech to us, to Lia. His grins are for her, his jokes are made while he holds her gaze. She holds my hand under the table and watches him with a small smile at the corner of her lips. After he introduces the new senator, he disappears behind the curtain. If we were at any other event, I'd lead Lia back there so we can start the real celebration. She looks too good to be wasted on everyone else. She needs to be between us, taking my orders and Enzo's worship. Her hand moves up my thigh like she knows exactly where my thoughts have gone. She keeps moving until she finds me hard under her palm, and then she just presses harder against me because she's evil incarnate tonight.

I almost reach out to stop her, but then I think better of it. She rubs against me through my pants, her fingers following my thickness until they reach my tip. I reach to grab her leg when she circles me through my pants. I pull at the fabric of her dress to bring it higher up her leg so my fingers can touch her skin. I don't take it further, just skim my fingers against the inside of her thigh and enjoy the feel of her hand on me. Enzo appears from somewhere; I stopped looking for him as I focused on what she was doing to me instead.

His hand falls on my shoulder in greeting and then brushes over the exposed skin of her back before he takes up the chair on her other side. "You came here on a mission tonight, Sunshine." He eyes her and then follows where her hand leads under the table. "Naughty girl," I can barely hear him as he whispers the words against her ear before he kisses her cheek.

I lean in to kiss her other cheek. It looks innocent enough

from the outside, but when my hand slips higher, it changes the kiss. "Naughty girls should get punished." I whisper against her other ear. She shivers under that promise, and Enzo and I make eye contact. It's time to go.

Enzo

It takes longer to leave than I would like. Seeing Lia when I stepped on the stage was like a punch to the throat. Seeing my fucking glorious woman smiling up at me, but out of my reach, was torture. She certainly came with a mission to drive Aren and I both nuts tonight, and it is working. Her dress hugs her and shows a teasing amount of skin and her hair is loose and wavy, begging to be wrapped around my wrist. We've fallen into a new way of life together this year. We've learned to read each other and see when we need space or time alone with Lia, but also when the door is open. Lia has her own room in both of the houses but usually ends up with both of us in bed with her, though there are nights one of us might go to our own room. But we work together and balance one another out.

Lia gets between us in the limo when we finally escape the building, and the driver keeps the separating window closed, as ordered. Lia practically climbs into my lap the moment the doors close. Her dress rides up high so she can spread her legs to either side of mine. "God damn, woman." I groan, my hands go to her hips and I move her against me.

"She's so cute when she thinks she's in control." Aren practically purrs.

"She can ride me until she gets exactly what she wants." I respond. I'm nearly one-hundred percent sure that she's not wearing any underwear, which means if I can get my button and zipper undone, I can be inside her in seconds. I start to lift her so I can do just that when Aren has to open his fucking mouth again.

"Lia, baby. Remember how you and Enzo teased me that first night? Remember how I watched while the two of you had your fun?" Lia looks away from me to give her attention to Aren. I see where this is going, and I don't like it. Fucking rude to cockblock a man about to bury himself deep in Lia's perfect pussy. "I think it's time Enzo got a taste of his own medicine, don't you? You wanted to have him look at you tonight. You wanted to tease him and make him starved for you. I don't think you've done a very good job. You gave in to him too easily. I think you can torture him better than that.

"Fuck you, Aren." I bite out.

"That is the idea." He grins at me and undoes his own pants. "Come on, baby, make him suffer." Lia goes right to him. She moves off my lap and sits on his instead. I might actually cry. All of her warmth and temptation was right there, and he stole it. "Do you want me inside you, Lia? Do you want Enzo to watch as I fuck you in the back of this car?"

"Yes, please."

"Please what?"

"Please, Daddy."

And he settles her down on his cock with those words. Calling him daddy dom was supposed to be an annoyance, but of course the bastard had to turn it in his favor. His groan of pleasure is enough to make me want to punch him right in the face. "Already so wet. Always so ready for us."

"Does that mean I'm your good girl?"

"Fuck no." He slaps the side of her thigh, which just makes her throw her head back with a moan. I take my cock out, needing some fucking relief. I won't make myself come, but I need some friction to relieve some of this pressure. "You are a naughty minx tonight who thinks she can take control. You should know better by now."

"Yet, I'm riding your dick." She grins and bounces on his lap. I don't think he has it in him tonight to go against her. She came to play tonight, and she's playing to win. That's my girl.

"Take what you need, Sunshine. Use him until you come." I order. Aren doesn't argue with me taking charge, so I do. "Look what you do to us. I'm so fucking hard I had to take my cock out. Do you want both of us when we get home? Are you going to be so good and take us both?"

"Oh, yes, please." She bounces to punctuate each word. "I want you both to fill me up."

"And you're going to take us so well. I'm going to watch our come drip down your legs when we're finished with you. But right now, I want you to come in the back of this limo. I want you to take everything you need from Aren like he's a battery powered toy. Let me watch you take. You look so fucking beautiful."

She puts her hands on Aren's shoulders and starts to really move her hips. His hand moves between her legs so he can brush against her clit. She doesn't tease, Lia listens, and she *takes*. It doesn't take long before she's coming, her mouth crashing against Aren's to muffle her moans. He keeps working her clit and deepens their kiss until he comes deep inside her. The two of them hold each other for another moment and then Aren seems to come back to himself. "Now you've taken what you want, but it's your turn to give. Get on your knees in the back of this car and suck Enzo off. He's suffered enough, don't you think?"

Okay, maybe I won't punch him in the face.

Lia

I'm still pulsing from my orgasm, but I quickly drop to the floor. My knees settle between Enzo's legs, his cock already standing high, begging for my mouth. The feel of his fingers in my hair sends a thrill through me. I've had these men worship me, I've had them edge me, and I've had them pamper me over this last year. They always seem to know what I want, what I need, and are always willing to fulfill those wishes. When Mara told me she and Zane were discussing the possibility of having a child, it got me thinking about a family. It was really the first time I thought of a future like that and I was terrified when I realized that wasn't something that I wanted. It was hard for me to approach my two men and tell them I didn't want children. I thought they'd insist or tell me I'd change my mind. Instead, both of them offered to get a vasectomy. They wanted me, and the three of us were enough family for them.

I bring Enzo's cock all the way to the back of my throat and hold him there, moving my tongue on the underside until his grip on my hair tightens. Aren gets down on the floor behind me and lifts my dress, exposing more of my body for Enzo to see. Aren's big hands brush over my breasts and gently twist my nipples until I bob my head in earnest, sucking Enzo like it's my sole purpose in life. They've given me everything. They've accepted everything about me and even opened my eyes to more things. I can at least return the favor when the opportunity presents itself.

We've all worked hard this past year, and tonight really seems to be the start of the next stage. I know so much more stands before us, but when I'm with them, everything else seems to fade away. Feeling Aren press behind me, the warmth of him reassuring as Enzo moves my head how he wants. I don't complain when tears come to my eyes and he settles at the back of my throat so that I have to swallow around him. Hearing him moan in pleasure is enough to keep me going. Feeling Aren's hands move over my exposed body is enough to make me feel safe.

They are my safe place. They are my home. And as Enzo comes down my throat and holds me there so that I take all of him, I just want to get back to our house so that we can do this all over again.

ACKNOWLEDGEMENTS

I had so much fun writing this duology. Thank you, Krissa and Jackie for listening to my crazy ideas and cheering me on along the way. I love you both dearly, and you are the bestest friends a girl could ask for!

Jackie, Krissa, and Nicole, thank you for being my first readers, helping with the editing process, and helping me clean up the story along the way!

Megan (@Graphitegeek) Thank you so much for another lovely cover! I always enjoy working with you, and you always make my vision come to life.

For my husband, thank you for building me a beautiful library and always supporting me.

Thank you, the reader, for picking up my book when there are so many choices out there. I hope I provided all the banter and spice your heart desired! I hope you fell in love with these characters like I did, and I hope you know how much I appreciate you for giving this indie author a chance!

Last but not least, a special shout-out to the indie bookstores that carry signed copies of our books! We love working with you, and I hope you get all the love and support that you deserve!

About the Author

Amanda Leigh is a book-hoarding dragon with a frozen coffee in one hand and a pen in the other. In school it was believed she was an avid note-taker, but she was really writing stories in those composition notebooks and avoiding math like the plague. When she's not making her characters suffer, she's helping them find love. She also co-writes fantasy under the pen name Dorian Moore.
Check out all her links and sign up for her newsletter at her website: www.dorianmoorebooks.com

Other Books:

Amanda Leigh:
Soul to Give
Revenge Next Door

Dorian Moore:
The Mystifying Series
Battle of Loinnir
Battle of Eloas
Battle of Skia